MOBJACK GAMBLE

MOBJACK MYSTERY & ADVENTURE SERIES
NUMBER 1

MOBJACK MYSTERY & ADVENTURE SERIES
BOOK 1

DON RICH

DON RICH

To the original core members of the Tropical Authors group, thanks, gang,
for letting me tag along and hang out with you.
—Don Rich

Library of Congress PCN Data

Rich, Don

Mobjack Gamble/Don Rich

Florida Refugee Press LLC

Cover by: Cover2Book.com

Published by FLORIDA REFUGEE PRESS LLC

Crozet, VA

Copyright © 2024 by Florida Refugee Press LLC

PREFACE

While this book, **Mobjack Gamble**, is listed as the first book in my **Mobjack Mystery and Adventure Series**, that's not exactly true. There is a prequel novella named **Mobjack Creek**, but don't look for it at your usual eBook retailers. Why? Because I'm giving it away for free. (You don't have to read the prequel to enjoy this book; I reintroduce all the characters in this book, but the prequel goes more in-depth, and free is free!)

Wait, WHAT? There has to be a catch somewhere! Nobody gives away stuff for free, right? Well...kind of. You get it for free when you sign up for my (also free) newsletter. Check it out at https://hello.donrichbooks.com/welcome/

I know, I know, you already receive 743 author newsletters, and you don't want another one showing up in your inbox every month. Well, I'll make you a deal, sign up for it, download your free prequel right away, and when the first newsletter issue arrives (usually around mid-month), just hit the little "Unsubscribe" link in the lower right at the bottom, and that's the last you'll see of these.

But I'm betting that if you read that first newsletter, you'll want to read the others each month. Why? Because there is good content in each one, not to mention you get a "heads-up" about discounts for my books. My newsletter readers get advance notice of new book presales at special lower rates a few days before those rates go up for everyone else. Plus, you get insight into the stories that inspire my stories (including photos).

So, sign up now before I come to my senses and start charging for **Mobjack Creek.** It isn't every day that you buy one book and get another one for free!

Now, flip the page and start enjoying this copy of **Mobjack Gamble!**

PROLOGUE

"Sheriff, it's definitely Billy. His wallet was in his pants, but his face was pretty messed up. There was some kinda trauma to the back of his skull, and the crabs did a number on him. But I recognized him, sure enough." The deputy assigned to Mathews County's marine patrol unit had dreaded making this call. He had responded to the report of a "floater" at the mouth of Mobjack Creek, at the place where it met Mobjack Bay. Fortunately, they didn't get this kind of call often.

Usually, when someone falls overboard and drowns, their lungs fill with water, and their body sinks to the bottom. Now, in the warmer months, that's where the cooler water is found, and it delays both the start as well as the ongoing process of decomposition. But the bottom is also where the Chesapeake Bay's famous blue crabs live, and Mobjack Bay is located on the western side of the Chesapeake. The scent of blood oozing from a wound in a body is like handing out an invitation for a free meal to the local crustacean population.

Once decomposition starts, gases start to build up in the tissues, and the body eventually rises to the surface. By then, many features are often distorted and discolored, making identification difficult.

Crab damage makes things just that much worse. And the longer the body is out of the water on warm summer days like today, the more pungent it becomes, making haste in identification very preferable.

Fortunately, there were enough facial features left intact for the deputy to make the identification as soon as he got the body aboard the boat. Billy Clifford was well known to the Sheriff's Department, both as a local methamphetamine dealer and user. Also, as a first cousin of Sheriff Timothy "Tiny" Clifford, the man who ensured that his cousin was protected from apprehension, much less prosecution. The Clifford family owned much of Mathews County and controlled the Board of Supervisors, Sheriff's Office, and all the County Administrative Offices. This was small-town nepotism, corruption, and politics at its worst.

The sheriff's voice was grave. Billy's lifestyle, occupation, and head trauma made him suspect this wasn't an accident. "Any bullet holes or stab wounds that you can see?"

"Nah, just that wound on the back of his skull, like somebody had hit him with somethin' heavy."

"Maybe like a dock," the sheriff muttered to himself, thinking back on an incident that had occurred yesterday.

"What's that, Sheriff?"

"Nothin'. Just get his body to the M.E. as fast as ya can. I wanna full autopsy done, an' I mean like yesterday."

"The M.E. is meetin' me at the boat ramp."

"Then what're ya doin' flappin' your gums on th' phone? Get movin'!"

The sheriff had a theory about what happened to his cousin and a suspect if his theory turned out to be right. Somebody he'd love to put handcuffs on, a smartass "come here." Meaning a non-native. Now, he just needed the Medical Examiner's autopsy findings so he could move forward.

In the meantime, Tiny knew he had a location to "sanitize." He headed for Mobjack Creek Marina and Billy's boat.

1

ACT CASUAL

I had a two-and-a-half-hour drive ahead of me. The first part was the easiest, as it was in the lower, flatter part of Virginia near the Chesapeake. There wasn't a whole lot of traffic on these rural roads. But once I reached the town of West Point, I knew traffic would start to pick up. Then, on I-64, it would become a no-holds-barred free-for-all, especially the short piece where it merged with I-95 going through Richmond. After the two roads split again on the far side, I'd continue westbound on I-64 to my destination of Crozet. This four-lane part of the interstate would still be busy, though not enough that I couldn't relax a bit and think. And did I ever have a lot to think about.

So this morning, I was looking forward to the solitude of the drive, all except that merged interstate section. I was returning from Mobjack Creek Marina, where three days ago, I had finalized the purchase of a boat—a twenty-five-year-old Sabre 36 Express. This in itself would have made it an eventful enough trip, though it turned out to be only one of several momentous events.

While there, I also managed to score a date with a very attractive, and now special-to-me, woman who was in her mid-thirties, as was I. Brandy McDonald was the head bartender at the Rivah Grill & Bar, a restaurant located at the marina. She was also my neighbor, living aboard her vintage houseboat in the slip next to mine. I'd met her almost two weeks ago when I'd first come over to look at the Sabre. Something had clicked between us that day when I'd stopped in for lunch.

Then, when I came back to complete the deal on the boat, I'd again gone to the bar for lunch and also to ask Brandy out. When I mentioned that she was attractive, that was a bit of an understatement. She's an inch or two shy of my own five foot ten, pretty, with long, dark-blond hair and dark-blue eyes. Her arms were toned from years of hauling and restocking cases of beer and kegs, and she had nicely shaped, medium-sized breasts and great legs. She also possessed a natural toughness and the ability to almost instantly and correctly size up a new customer. Both of these traits had served her well as an attractive woman bartending in a waterfront bar. It was not normally a rough place, though my second visit had its moments. I'd gotten a big lesson that day on the Clifford family.

"Tiny" Clifford was the sheriff. He'd spotted me as I'd driven through the little town of Mathews on my way to the marina. I was in my "retro-mod" white 1991 Jeep Wrangler YJ, the rare Islander edition with square headlights. I'd swapped the old straight six-cylinder engine a few years back for a fuel-injected small-block V8 with much more than just stock horsepower.

Even though I was obeying the town's speed limit, the low rumble of that powerful engine had caught Tiny's attention as I'd driven past where he was writing someone a ticket. He looked up at me as I passed, giving me a creepy feeling that it wouldn't be the last time I'd be seeing him. I was right. A while later, he showed up at the marina as I was having lunch at the dockside bar. He'd come to run his cousin Billy out of the marina before he and another cousin, Ted Clifford, could show the property to a group of investors. Billy was a methamphetamine dealer and addict, as well as a known troublemaker. The last thing they needed now was Billy causing trouble and screwing up the showing.

Ted was the Chairman of the Board of Supervisors and the county's biggest developer. He wanted to transform the marina and boat-yard into a condominium project, the first of its kind in the county. The fact that he didn't own the property at the time didn't dissuade him at all; he had a plan for taking care of that, too.

Tiny came over to me at the bar, giving me his "I'm the law around here" speech and warning me not to get out of line with my "hot rod." Whatever. I wasn't impressed. I continued talking with Brandy as Tiny walked down the dock to Billy's boat. Tiny came back past the bar a few minutes later, headed for the parking lot to await Ted's arrival. Then on his way out, Billy showed up at the bar feeling brave and bulletproof; side effects from the chunk of crystal meth he'd just smoked before leaving his boat. He had become obsessed with Brandy, and in his chemical fog, he decided that today was his day to convince her to "party" with him.

Brandy kept edging down the bar toward me, trying to get away from Billy. Unfortunately, this meant he ended up standing beside me. Unlike Brandy, I didn't have the luxury of having a bar top separating us. The guy reeked of a plethora of body odors. These ranged from halitosis to stale sweat and foot, underarm, and crotch odors, all of which stemmed from a severe lack of personal hygiene. This was common among "tweakers," meaning habitual meth users. I didn't think he'd had a shower in at least a week. Maybe two.

I was now in danger of revisiting what had originally been a very delicious lunch, so I told the guy he reeked and that I needed him to give me some breathing space. But the thing about tweakers is they're unpredictable and prone to violence. I never saw the fist coming that connected with the side of my head, knocking me off my barstool onto the wood dock. I did, however, see the shoe that was now aiming for my rib cage. I grabbed it and yanked him off balance, sending him crashing down onto that same wood surface, his head making a sound not unlike that of a bat connecting with a baseball for a home run.

Tiny had seen this from the parking lot and raced back over. Instead of arresting his cousin, he then threatened to arrest me. He only backed off after Cam Thomas, the property and business owner, came out of his office saying that his security cameras had captured and recorded the whole thing and that I'd been the one who was attacked. Tiny then sent Billy on his way and warned me to stay out of trouble.

Cam was the polar opposite of Tiny. Within a second or two of meeting Tiny, I'd already disliked him for years. But on the other hand, I felt like Cam and I had been pals for decades. Little did I know then that we would become much closer friends and allies against the Cliffords before that day ended.

After Tiny met with Ted in the parking lot, he returned to the bar and served Cam with a notice that the Cliffords had bought and were now calling the loan that was collateralized by the marina, restaurant, and boatyard. The property was worth a little over four million dollars, and the note was for two million and change. Cam had thirty days to come up with the cash or lose the place, including that extra two million in equity. He freaked out.

Boatyards are notorious for having environmental issues that must be mitigated before any bank would lend money on one of these properties. Because of this, Cam's note was from a private "lender of last resort" that had come with a high interest rate. He and his siblings inherited the place when their parents died. He needed cash to buy out his sister and brother, who had no interest in the businesses or the property. Ted Clifford had approached them about purchasing the property to put up multi-story condos. Cam's siblings had given him thirty days to come up with the money, or they would accept Clifford's offer, with or without his approval.

Cam's lender had been the only one considering lending on the property and still meeting the deadline. Now, the lender had sold the note to the Cliffords, undoubtedly at a much higher price than its face value. Cam thought he had nowhere left to turn. He was crushed by the news and resigned to losing the businesses. He was about to find out he was wrong.

Something happened to me when I first saw this place just shy of two weeks ago. While my Sabre first drew me here, I quickly became attached to the location. Because of this, I made certain that the prepaid annual slip had been transferred in the deal along with the boat's title. Mobjack Creek was different from any of the other marinas I'd visited in Virginia. For one thing, it was quiet and secluded, far up the creek and near its headwaters. The pool, the restaurant, and the outside dock bar on the premises were all pluses. Then, of course, there was Brandy.

So, I liked things just the way they were, but in an instant, the Cliffords threatened to take it all away from me and everyone else who kept their boats here. Then I talked Cam into taking a ride with me on my boat, where I pitched him an idea. I'd buy half the marina for that two million and change, becoming a mostly silent partner.

He was initially skeptical until I repeatedly pointed out that this was the only way for him to save his business. Plus, he'd lose his largest monthly expense, those loan payments. Meaning there would be a lot more profit at the bottom line each month than there had been, even after splitting it with me. Then, I explained why I was so willing to help. I had a lot of reasons, not the least of which was that I hated seeing the Cliffords win. I also didn't want to have my boat in the middle of a construction zone for the next year or so only to end up with dozens of "condo commandos" staring down at me from their lofty perches.

Finally, Cam agreed to the deal. We celebrated over dinner, and then I returned to my boat to relax with a movie before hitting my bunk. Somewhere during the flick, I heard sounds of a struggle next door on Brandy's houseboat. I raced over there in the semi-darkness, finding an extremely high Billy Clifford preparing to sexually assault Brandy. He'd thrown her against the exterior bulkhead, stunning her and ripping open her top. I pulled him away and fought with him.

During the fight, I accidentally shoved Billy through a rotten spot in the houseboat's wooden side railing. He then hit his head against the edge of a steel "H" column next to the boat, which supported the dock's roof. The impact caved in the back of his skull. I'm pretty sure he was dead before he hit the water and then disappeared beneath the surface. No way was I going in after his body. Instead, I tended to Brandy, who wouldn't let me call the paramedics or the Sheriff's

Office, saying that Tiny would arrest both of us. After my earlier scuffle at the bar, I knew she was right. I decided to leave Billy's body where it was, knowing that the tides and the currents would probably move it without any help from me.

Brandy's houseboat door key had broken off in the lock at some point during the attack and ensuing struggle. I'd need some daylight and a few tools to open it and fix the lock. Meanwhile, I took her to my boat to ice the knot, which was rising on the back of her head. I was also concerned that she might have a concussion. She suggested that I could watch her closely if she stayed there with me.

Brandy had seen that it was really hitting me hard that I'd just killed a man. A very bad man, to be sure, and it had been an accident, but that didn't change the outcome. My hands had begun to shake uncontrollably, something she'd noticed since she was holding them. But hers were rock steady, despite having come so close to being raped. That's when she shared a secret she'd never shared with anyone else ever before. It gave me great insight as to just how tough this woman was.

Two years prior, she'd been attacked on her way home late at night from her old job in Mathews. She'd been forced off the main road over onto a deserted side road by one of Tiny's deputies. He'd claimed she was speeding excessively, and she was going to jail if she wouldn't have sex with the guy right there. When she said she'd rather go to jail, he shoved her back across the console and began choking her while simultaneously yanking down her shorts and ripping off her panties. She managed to reach under her seat and grab her stun gun, zapping him in the balls after he'd pulled his own pants down. She hit him again in the neck, then shoved him back out through the open car door. He fell flat on his back in the road.

Tiny passed by over on the main road and spotted their taillights down the dark side road. He turned around to investigate, and when he pulled up, it was obvious what had happened. But he chose to send the deputy on his way after he regained his senses. Then he handcuffed Brandy, leaving her standing next to her car with her shorts still down around her ankles while he carefully collected the stun gun. He preserved her fingerprints and the deputy's DNA on it by placing the device in an evidence bag. He told her that if she said anything about what happened that night to anyone, he'd make sure she was charged with a felony and that she'd get five years in prison.

She quit her job in town and went to work for Cam at the marina bar so she wouldn't have to stray far from the marina after dark alone. It turned out to be a wise move, as that deputy tried the same tactic a month later on another woman, a waterman's wife. She stabbed him with a fillet knife in his thigh and then escaped. Unfortunately for the deputy, she turned out to be a distant Clifford cousin —but a Clifford nonetheless. The deputy disappeared that night after being treated and released from the emergency room. Brandy said this was just the way things were in Mathews County. So, I understood even more why she was so reluctant to call the authorities, and I followed her lead.

We held and comforted each other that night like two people who had just shared a common traumatic experience, albeit for different reasons. Somewhere in the night, that comfort became sex as we sought solace in each other's arms, replacing that bad memory with something much more pleasant. Then, despite a couple of initial awkward moments in the harsh light of the following morning, we realized that the two of us now shared a unique bond. However, we didn't know how the previous night would affect our new friendship in the long term. But over breakfast, we discovered a nice level of comfort between us, realizing that neither of us wanted what happened last night to turn out to be just a one-night stand. It wasn't. After spending her day off together and having a great first-date dinner, we ended up back at my boat, taking up where we'd left off the night before.

It sounds weird to have acted so casually after the events that happened on the houseboat. Don't judge Brandy harshly, or me for that matter. She had found in me an ally who wasn't afraid to help defend her against the Cliffords. This came after two years of feeling totally alone and isolated, unable or unwilling to share with anyone else anything about that first attack. I'd become her first and only confidant, and this gave us a level of closeness that could have otherwise taken weeks, if not months, to reach, if ever.

We knew that at some point, Billy's body would surface and be discovered. If we had been acting strange between now and then, and his death was ruled anything but an accident, we'd undoubtedly be pegged as suspects by Tiny, especially after our interactions with Billy at the bar the day before.

Remember how I said Brandy was tough? If you didn't know, you'd never guess that she'd been attacked by how she was acting. Though she'd had a lot of practice over the last two years. But I knew from that first night together she and I were both holding a lot of emotions inside, only sharing them with each other. At least we each had that outlet, which was much more than she'd had in dealing with the incident with that deputy.

2

TOO MUCH CASH

On the drive back, I started mulling over some of the decisions I'd made and thought hard to try to find answers to the challenges that still lay before me. I was thankful for the light traffic.

There was another reason I wanted to partner up with Cam on the marina besides that of keeping the status quo. I had two businesses that threw off an embarrassingly large amount of cash, mostly because they were illegal and untaxed. Over the years, I had grown to become the largest moonshiner in Virginia. Then, I added regularly scheduled high-stakes poker games and one of the biggest underground poker tournaments on the East Coast at my sporting club. It was now literally underground, but I'll get to that in a minute. The moonshine and poker operations were strictly cash businesses and probably better described as "cash cows."

I'd been able to launder enough of that moonshine cash at first to be able to finance my legitimate craft brewery and expand the moonshine operation. Then, I bought my sporting club property from a railroad after some journalists discovered that it was actually a front for one of the government's secret presidential bomb shelters. This one was tucked into Bucks Elbow Mountain in Crozet. They "outed" it soon after they'd done the same thing to the larger congressional bomb shelter over at the Greenbrier Resort in West Virginia. Massive amounts of tax dollars went down the drain after both exposés, but those reporters didn't care; they had gotten their headlines.

I bought the bomb shelter property for roughly the value of raw land. It helped that the government's cover story for all the initial construction activity there was due to it being a polluted Superfund site. This had scared off any other interest in the property. By then, I had figured out the whole Superfund thing was totally false. After buying the property, I cranked up the club business in the preexisting lodge buildings, which had been built as a functional cover, much like the Greenbrier had for its substantially larger congressional shelter. I began connecting my members with the area's best hunting and fishing guides, and the word quickly spread among many wealthy Virginians.

In addition to a few accommodations in the previously secret subterranean bomb shelter, the lodge had numerous above ground guest rooms for out-of-town members. We also had a nice-sized dining room, a bar, and a commercial kitchen. I added a number of large, covered, open-air exterior patio dining areas. These were equipped with tables, fireplaces, and bars. Some were also set up as laid-back exterior living rooms with plush, high-end patio furniture.

These patios were all connected by walkways and were perfect for more casual private parties of up to a couple hundred people during the more temperate months. They could also be rented out individually for smaller get-togethers. I added large, brick, open-fire cooking pits and smokers that I had built into a screened building set back against the woods. We held monthly ranch-style dinners for the club members on those patios. These featured a variety of smoked and open-pit-cooked prime meats, all prepared in that screened building.

For the growing DC member group, the whole experience was far from what they were used to up there on the usual "rubber chicken circuit." I think the club's patio dinners and dark wood interior accents were what attracted so many of the "inside the Beltway" crowd. Excellent food and drinks in an atmosphere that was casual, rustic, yet chic. And "chic" came with a hefty price.

Only a small fraction of the members were aware of the card games that took place in the bomb shelter on certain nights of each month. Of course, there was also the clandestine annual poker tournament; the last one was held a month ago. It kept getting larger and richer than ever. Which also meant my cut was growing at the same rate. But as my illicit businesses grew and threw off even more cash, I couldn't spend it all without attracting unwanted attention. It was a nice problem to have at times, but a problem nonetheless.

I was careful not to flash around too much cash. My boat wasn't a big new yacht; it was older and smaller by today's standards. Not unlike what you might expect that someone with a successful small business might have. My Jeep was also old; you could only tell there had been a ton of cash put into it if you looked very closely and knew what you were looking at. I didn't own an airplane, and I wasn't into jewelry other than my vintage Rolex MilSub watch. Once again, you'd have to know what you were looking at to realize it cost twice what my boat did. It was a stainless watch, not solid gold like so many other Rolexes, with a black face instead of one of the popular bright colors. And instead of a metal watch band, it came with a nylon strap. At a distance, it didn't even appear to be what you'd expect a Rolex to look like. But watch aficionados knew, and more than one did a double take when they spotted it. Unicorns are more common than MilSubs.

So, cash had been piling up in my safe, and it was all at risk if the ATF or the IRS came calling. The time had now come to make some changes. I wanted to sell the moonshine business, but I hadn't found anyone who could afford it and had somewhere safe to move it to.

Some years ago, I bought a large, defunct food-processing plant in downtown Crozet for pennies on the dollar and used it to create my craft brewery and bar. But I also built a secret room inside the building that housed my distillery, which would be difficult to recreate elsewhere.

The fermentation of the mash and the eventual distillation in the quantities we produced each had distinct odors. It was tough to hide them. However, when mixed in with the somewhat similar odor of brewing beer, they weren't that noticeable. Most of the risk with my operation came in transporting and distributing the finished product. However, I had a loyal and close-mouthed group of distributors that I built up over the years. They'd no more give me up to the revenuers than I would them. Though we were all taking our chances, that was an accepted part of the business.

Now, though, I was looking to eliminate a lot of the risk associated with both of my cash businesses, not just the moonshine. This brings me to the sporting club and its poker business. One of my players, actually, my biggest player—in status, not size—was Alex Phipps, a DC power broker. It was whispered that he'd put many senators and even the last four presidents in their offices. He was like the "Don" of Washington, DC politics. And Alex had told me several times that he'd love to throw in with me on the Buck's Elbow Sports Club and its associated secret games. Until two days ago, I'd always politely turned him down. That was before I met any of the Cliffords.

I was in a unique position. I made more now with my legitimate businesses than I needed in order to keep living the lifestyle I'd carved out. However, the risk of discovery and prosecution of the less-than-legal side has increased steadily in proportion to my cash income. I took as many precautions as possible; I even had the Crozet sheriff on a cash retainer. The truth is, even that wasn't as simple as it sounds.

Sheriff Steve Chesney was a few years older than me, but as native Crozetians, we shared more than one common bond. We went to the same public grade schools, and we'd both watched sadly as the town's population had grown by five hundred percent over the past twenty years. Outsiders now far outnumbered us natives.

Steve tipped me off and kept me from being busted more than once when I was starting out in the moonshine business. We were friends, and he knew I was struggling to get started and that it was more or less a victimless crime. He also knew that what I was making was the best 'shine you could get anywhere in the area, probably because he was also one of my customers.

After the first time Steve warned me the ATF was snooping

around, I never charged him for any moonshine from that point on. While my business and income grew, I learned that he had a young daughter with significant health issues and mounting medical costs. But I didn't learn that from him; he wasn't the kind of person to complain.

The next time he stopped by to pick up a couple of jars, there were a couple of bundles of cash in the paper bag as well. He got mad when he found them, saying he only warned me because we were friends. He said he wasn't going on the take for anybody. I told him I knew this and that I wasn't asking him for any additional favors. I said that this was simply interest on a debt that I felt I owed him, and it didn't have to do with anything he might choose to do for me from then on. And that the only reason I'd added it in was because we were indeed friends, and I could finally afford to pay him back.

At first, he looked like he might hit me, but then I saw him mull it over and finally nod. He knew he'd crossed that line when he first learned about my business and didn't do anything. While that may have made him a bad cop, it didn't make him a bad person, at least in my eyes. He went out of his way to help people, whether on duty or not. And he knew there would always be a market for moonshine; it's a Southern cultural thing. Rastafarians have their ganja, and we Southerners have our moonshine.

Steve also knew there was a lot of moonshine out there that wasn't safe and could do severe harm to anyone who drank it. He knew that I'd never make anything like that. So, from his viewpoint, it was better to leave my operation alone and go after the toxic ones that were hurting people.

Steve was my first line of defense, especially for moonshine. However, those poker games had different security challenges. I had to be very careful who I let play and who knew about it. The dealers, bartenders, and servers who worked the games were my best people, all well paid, in cash. This was a totally separate crew from the rest of those who worked at the lodge. Those folks were unaware of the games' existence. This separation was yet another layer of security.

Something else in my favor was the higher stature of my players, especially Alex. However, by him only being a player, this might mean there was cover for himself and maybe some of his fellow players, but not the organization and me. Taking him on as a partner would change this. Many of his contacts could squelch any investigation or indictment that might be headed our way. A prime example of DC power politics at its finest.

As I said, up until this point, I'd resisted taking him on as a partner—him or anybody else, for that matter. However, stumbling into Mobjack Creek changed my thinking in a number of ways. I wanted to be able to spend increasing amounts of time down there, relaxing. I had great people who could handle ninety percent of my business in Crozet, and it was time to let them do just that. The realization that I needed to help Cam save the marina and restaurant business was also a game changer for me. It gave me a purpose for being down there other than to just sit on my ass.

Suddenly, the idea of partnering with Alex seemed very attractive. Not just for the cover he could bring to the operation, but he had access to piles of clean cash, and I needed two million clean and very traceable bucks in a damn hurry. In one phone call, he agreed to front me the money, and in exchange, I offered him forty-nine percent of the club, including its "off-book" activities. He would end up with that same percentage of the profits, including the unreported cash. While I had limited places I could safely spend it, he could utilize his cut for, well, let's just call it "political grease"—transactions that didn't require receipts. So, in those situations, having untraceable cash was a nice benefit of our new association.

While I was swapping mostly equal equity in two businesses, I'd be gaining a nice, clean income stream from Mobjack Creek. It wasn't as much as the games threw off, but it was money I could spend anywhere without worrying about the IRS. I was tired of worrying about them and the ATF with my moonshine...and that's when the solution hit me. I was around mile marker 181 on I-64, forty-five minutes outside Crozet, when I decided not to sell my moonshine operation; I'd take it legit instead. I had a great production setup, a seasoned distiller, and recipes we'd worked on perfecting for years.

I'd have to collect taxes on each bottle, of course, and that would turn a lot of my regular customers off. But just as I'd built up the business illegally by letting the product's quality speak for itself, it should be able to compete on the shelves of the state-owned liquor stores.

By the time I'd reached the foothills just east of Charlottesville, I already had an action plan put together in my head. I couldn't wait to get to Crozet and spring this on my crew. No more having to ship the product out in the dead of night in unmarked panel vans and sourcing supplies from several different places to keep from drawing too much attention. This was going to be a challenge, but one of a different kind. And it should be fun. Fifteen more miles to go, and I couldn't wait.

3

CROZET

I got off I-64 in Charlottesville, then went west on Route 250. I hopped onto Route 240 via the roundabout, just past a popular local dive and watering hole named Farduners. The start of Route 240 was a curving, narrow, steeply inclined road that led up into Crozet. My transplanted V8 merely purred as my Jeep tackled the grade. The canopy of huge, overhanging oak and maple trees made this section of road dark and much cooler than it was after it leveled off, becoming a wide-open plateau at the town limits. The average elevation in Crozet is about 875 feet above sea level, and up on the mountain at the club, we're at about 1,250.

One of the last remaining farms within the town limits was now off to my right; the acreage split about fifty-fifty between cattle and alternating crops of hay and corn. I saw the tall green stalks had begun to "tassel," signaling they'd reached full height and had begun spreading their pollen, fertilizing the field. That farm was a beautiful sight—wonderful green space on gently rolling hills, with the town reservoir on its eastern border and the Blue Ridge Mountains vista to the west. Views like this were why so many people want to move here and are now clogging our roads.

To handle the influx of new people, several large developments had been built on the left (south) side of the road. Hundreds of houses were now crammed together in the space where a hundred cattle had grazed not two decades earlier. In their "wisdom" some twenty-five years ago, the local politicos had designated sleepy little Crozet as the "growth area" of the county. At the time, there were around two thousand of us Crozetians, most of whom were employed at the local food-processing plant or on the farms. The politicos wanted to be able to control the county's growth "sensibly" and came up with this as a solution. But they promised at the time that the higher-density zoning would be limited to south of 240 and north of 250, affecting only a dozen or so of the area's family farms.

Do you know how you can tell when a politician is lying? Their lips are moving. Though I can't judge them too harshly in this case. They had built a large sewer and water plant to handle the increasing needs of that food-processing plant, and they'd issued some very large municipal bonds to do it. Then, with no notice, the corporation that owned the plant moved the production to a newer, more modern plant in another state. Crozet lost its major employer and its source of revenue for the water plant almost overnight. It was the equivalent of a localized Great Depression. A new income stream had to be created to repay those bonds, or the county would be forced to default. As they analyzed the situation, this excess available water capacity now doomed those bucolic farms.

The more than ten thousand new people who moved to Crozet since then quickly absorbed that excess water and sewer capacity and created the need for yet another water plant expansion. Of course, why would you only build what you need when it would never be this cheap again to build something larger to encourage even more development? Once again faced with excess water capacity, the "powers that be" began to approve more developments quietly, but this time on the north side of Route 240.

As soon as this happened, I knew the beautiful view across the corn and cattle fields I loved was now on borrowed time. Progress was what they liked to call it, but unconscionable sprawl was more my term. This was yet another reason that I wanted to help Cam with the marina. The fight against development here in Crozet was already lost. But it was just getting started at Mobjack Creek, and I wanted to be part of the resistance.

I slowed as I approached the original part of town, where the speed limit stairstepped down quickly. I hit the beginning of the twenty-five-mile-per-hour stretch, which started right in front of my brewery. Our bar was located at the far end of the building. I saw that Lana, my bar manager, had the glass garage doors open in front of the long counter that looked out over the patio and the road. The bar floor was about five feet higher than the patio and the street, making for a nice, elevated view for our patrons. I tapped my horn as I passed by and saw her wave from behind the service bar in the center of the room.

Just past the brewery, a pair of train tracks came into view and now bordered the road on the left side, across from a handful of small houses that faced the railroad. These homes had been built by and for some of those factory workers so many decades ago. As I continued toward the roughly two-block downtown section, those houses gave way to our volunteer fire department station. After that came an older strip center with stores selling everything from groceries to auto parts. Another handful of old buildings beyond this held a couple of restaurants and bars, plus a yoga studio and insurance office, and that was about the length of it. Our downtown was the kind of place where you didn't want to blink, or you'd miss it, even at twenty-five miles per hour.

On my left, just before the old train station that had now been transformed into an artist's gallery, was a train track siding. It normally had a few track maintenance machines stored there, though it was strangely empty now. Just ahead beyond the only four-way stop in town was a gas station, the last commercial property on this road. Then came another half mile of very old, smaller homes facing across the narrow two-lane to the railroad. Finally, the tracks curved out of sight to my left, heading for the famous 150-year-old Crozet tunnel that had been bored through Afton Mountain. Now, both sides of the road had given way to greenspace. Cattle, sheep, horses, and alpacas grazed on either side in lush, green fields, some on steep hills.

Now, literally at the base of the Blue Ridge Mountains, the road began curving and climbing again as it narrowed even further. Like the area down by the marina, the older farmhouses were now getting displaced by new mini-manses; their former gravel drives were now being replaced by asphalt and stamped concrete. Pickup trucks were becoming a smaller portion of the road's traffic, exchanged mostly for expensive foreign and domestic SUVs and sports cars. More evidence of the money that was pouring into the area.

After a few more miles, I slowed and made a left turn into the Buck's Elbow Sports Club's driveway. Weathered brick gateposts with bronze plaques bearing the club's name and "Members Only" stood on either side of the entrance.

My Jeep climbed the sloping and curving asphalt drive that wound through the trees until the main lodge and the patio outbuildings came into view. Several members' cars were in the parking area on the left, their owners undoubtedly having lunch or getting a start on an early cocktail hour.

I kept driving, pulling behind the main building into the employee parking lot, though I didn't park there. I hit the button on an opener for a garage door on the side of the building. It opened not to a small garage but a cavernous parking area built to handle dozens of vehicles from a large motorcade. Keeping those cars out of sight was part of the security plan when this facility served the president. Now, it had become part of the security for my poker operation. The regular players, all big hitters, had been issued their own openers so they could park here while playing. Just another one of the perks of my games. This way, none of the non-playing members would spot a player's car and wonder where they were, and what they were up to. The tunnel opening leading to the shelter's massive steel blast door was over in the far-right corner of the room.

As I turned toward my reserved space in the opposite corner to the left, I spotted Parker Phipps's new car in the space next to mine. There was no mistaking it since it was the only red Ferrari F8 around here. But I was used to seeing it parked out in front, along with the other members' cars, since Parker didn't have her own door opener. At least, she hadn't had one up until now. Her father must've loaned her his.

Parker was the slight...complication...that came with the deal. She had been chasing after me for quite a while, but I'd been able to turn her down, saying that because her father was one of my largest club members, and I didn't want to lose his business if things didn't work out between us. The real truth was that she was not my type. Not even close. But I didn't want to insult her and lose her father's business by telling her that.

Parker was twenty-seven, a drop-dead gorgeous, short-haired platinum blonde, and used to getting what she wanted from the men in her life, including her father. Take that Ferrari, for instance. It cost a third of a million dollars. Her father also bought her the county's largest winery and conference center in the small town next to Crozet called Whitehall. Phipps Estate Vineyards was a huge property. It cost Alex almost ten times what I was selling him half of the sporting club for, but Parker wanted it, and her father wanted to make her happy.

Like I said, Parker wasn't my type, and I knew how things would end if she were. After a while, she'd tire of introducing me to her friends as her father's business associate or that guy who owns the sporting club in little old Crozet. Then she'd meet another guy on one of her trips down to Palm Beach, and suddenly I'd get ghosted. No thanks. I think the only reason she had a thing for me was because I was an interesting trinket that wasn't for sale. Nobody ever told her "no," and that was eating her alive. She wanted what she couldn't have. Like the clicker. I'd told her several times that the garage was only for my high-roller players. But if Alex had given her his, so be it. That's not a battle I wanted to fight at the outset of our partnership.

Instead of going toward the bomb shelter, I went through a door next to my parking space. The hallway beyond it was lined with doors leading to the laundry, my apartment, and my office. The door at the far end led into the lodge's bar. After dropping off the bag with my boat clothes and sheets in the laundry, I went to my office. I texted Hitch, asking him to come in.

Sam "Hitch" Hitchings was my second-in-command and one of the main reasons I could take a few days off over at Mobjack Creek. There was almost nothing that I could do that he couldn't do as well. Hitch had just turned thirty, but he had the seasoned ability of someone ten or fifteen years older. He was so good that my phone never rang during these last three days because he had everything under control. Or so I'd thought.

Hitch came into my office looking like he was under a storm cloud. It was not what I expected since the guy was always so positive and upbeat.

I asked, "What's wrong?"

"Danny, you've always been up front with me until now. I thought you'd at least have given me a heads-up before you sold the place so I could have something else lined up in case I didn't like the new owner, which, by the way, I don't."

"Whoa! What the hell field is this coming out of? New owner? I'm still the majority owner, and I thought you liked Alex!"

"You didn't sell the place to Parker?"

"Hell no! I sold forty-nine percent to her father. It was a spur-of-the-moment kind of thing. I haven't even signed the papers yet, and I wanted to tell you in person before I did."

"Well, Parker must've missed that memo. She blew in here like a hurricane this morning, issuing orders to the staff and telling me to program a garage opener for her. She's out in the dining room, introducing herself to the members as the new owner."

I took a deep breath to try and calm myself. No way I wanted to know what my blood pressure was right now. "I'll handle her, Hitch. I knew there would be some 'Parker complications' with this deal, but I had expected them to be personal ones. I didn't think they'd be falling on you."

Hitch chuckled and smiled. "I wouldn't want to be in your shoes right now."

"No, you wouldn't want to be in *Parker's*. She won't like what I'm about to tell her."

"Want me to ask her to come in here, Danny?"

I shook my head. "No, I'll handle her myself. And I won't be asking, I'll be telling."

I waited three minutes after Hitch returned to the dining room before I followed him in. He was right; Parker was going from table to table, chatting up the members. I walked over to her, and she put on a big smile and then tried putting an arm around me. I wasn't having any of it. I sidestepped her and then roughly pulled her away by the elbow, steering her to my office.

After I closed the door behind us, she said, "What the hell, Danny? You can't go leading me around like a horse. That's no way to treat your partner!"

"My partner? *You* are not my partner! I don't want you telling people that you are either a partner and certainly not the owner. I hadn't even told my people about the deal yet. Your father was going to be my partner, but right now, I'm calling that off."

I saw a momentary flicker of panic in her eyes before she recovered and said, "Well, I handle our family's properties around here, and you can't call it off. He said you were in a rush and needed that money right away. It should have hit your bank account already, so now our deal is done."

"No, I haven't signed any paperwork yet, and he and I agreed that was a personal loan until I do. But I will happily repay that loan and keep the whole club to myself without any partners." I was bluffing, since, without Alex's cash, I didn't have the two million on hand to buy into the marina, even including all of my unlaundered cash.

Parker didn't seem to know how to respond to that, and she stood there silently as she absorbed it and tried to figure out what to do next. I walked behind my desk and sat in my chair while she thought things over. Unfortunately for her, she chose the wrong tactic to come back at me with.

"Well then, I'll tell my father we'll have to take our business elsewhere. In fact, maybe we'll start our own card games and tournaments at my vineyards." Parker crossed her arms for emphasis, trying to look both imposing as well as serious.

"You could certainly do that. Just make sure to give that garage opener back to Hitch on your way out."

"Wait, what? Give it back? On my way out?"

I nodded solemnly. "Well...yeah. You didn't think you could threaten to go into competition with me and then have you and your father still remain members here, did you? That's not going to happen. I'll call Alex and let him know I'll be wiring the money back this afternoon, that our deal is off, and you two are no longer welcome around here since you are going to be my competition." I pulled my phone out of my pocket and opened the contacts page.

"Hold on, Danny; I didn't say we would; I was just tossing out an idea. I know I can speak for my father when I say we don't want out of the deal."

"An idea or a threat? That's the thing, Parker, you can't speak for your father, at least not to me. You were never part of the deal." I called Alex and put the call on speaker.

Alex picked up on the first ring. "Hello, Danny. Is everything on track?"

Parker had raced around my desk and now yanked my phone out of my hand. "Everything is fine, Daddy; Danny accidentally butt-dialed you. I'll call you later." With that, she hung up the phone.

I grabbed the phone, but she still hung onto it with one hand.

"Don't ever grab my phone again, Parker," I said as I yanked it away from her.

"I was saving you from making a terrible mistake, Danny. My father respects you, and he only respects a handful of people. That's not something you want to throw away because you could never get it back again if you did."

"Nice try. You mean you're saving your own ass. If he knew how you disrupted things here this morning, he'd be furious. Do you know one of the biggest reasons he wants to own part of this place? It's because of how well it's run. And because he knows he'll never have to get involved in its operation to ensure that it stays running smoothly. So there's no way that he would ever have given you a green light to come barging in here."

"Please don't call him." Her original look of confidence had faded. "I just wanted us to run this together, Danny, and get closer to each other in the process."

"That's not going to happen, Parker. If you leave now, I can start repairing the damage with my staff. Thanks to your little stunt, they think I deceived them and sold out completely without telling them first. I don't want to have you here as a distraction while I'm meeting with them."

"But I get to keep my garage access." It was partly a question and partly a statement. After everything she stirred up this morning, by rights, I should take it back, but that would only serve to further embarrass and humiliate her. As much as she'd pissed me off, she was still the only child of my friend and now partner.

"Yeah, sure. But use it to get out of here so I can start fixing things."

Relief washed across her face, and without another word, she turned and headed out the door, closing it softly behind her. What I didn't see but knew for certain was on her face right now was a small smile of victory in the battle over the clicker.

After having dealt with Parker over these last few years, I knew that by letting her keep the clicker, she would save just enough face to be content for now. If she'd have left without it, there would've been more of her crap to shovel, which I didn't need right now. I knew this wasn't the last time I'd bump heads with her.

I texted Hitch and told him I wanted to hold a quick staff meeting after the last table cleared out after lunch. I'd just sent the message when my phone rang. It was Alex.

"Is Parker still there?"

"No. She just left."

"Do you want to tell me what was behind that call a few minutes ago?"

"Not particularly. I handled the situation."

"Situation? Do I need to..."

"If you did, I'd say you're buying into the wrong place."

Alex waited a few seconds, then said, "It's a tough age she's at, Danny. It can be harder for some than for others."

"Alex, she's no teenager, at least chronologically. And I can handle her, so don't worry."

"So, our deal is still on track?"

"Absolutely. The papers were waiting for me when I got back. I'll sign them this afternoon and send them to your office. We can file them with the county next week."

"Keep them there. I'm coming down to the vineyards this afternoon and staying through the weekend. Do you have time for dinner tonight?"

"Sure."

"Good. I'll see you there around seven thirty."

"I'll look forward to it."

4

A MAJOR COUP

Hitch texted me, *Danny, somebody out here wants to see you.*
Who is it?

I don't know. Never seen her before. But she's really upset.

About?

*Said something about James Hunter being her fiancé? I don't know, but
I need to get her out of the bar; she's almost hysterical.*

I frowned, then replied, *Okay. My office.*

I came out from behind my desk just as the young woman
entered the room. She appeared to be in her early twenties and could
easily have been described as stunning if her tears hadn't made such
a mess of her makeup. Her hair was unbrushed, and her eyes were
red with slight bags underneath. She looked like she hadn't slept in
days.

I held out my hand. "I'm Danny Reynolds. How can I help you,
Miss..."

She took my hand, and then, in between sobs, she managed to
say, "P...Patti Edwards. I...I'm so sorry; I didn't know what else to do."

I motioned for her to sit in a guest chair while I leaned back
against the front of my desk. "What is this about?"

"My...fiancé. James Hunter."

I smiled and said, "I'm guessing you mean Jimmy Junior, not James Senior. What about him?"

She nodded and sniffled. "He was here last night, playing cards, and lost the money his father gave us for our honeymoon. When his father finds out, he'll be furious with James. He told him that he had a problem and that if he didn't quit gambling, he'd fire him and then cut him off without a cent. James has gone through everything we have, Mr. Reynolds; I didn't know where else to turn.

"Last night was the final straw. James is sick; he can't stop. If his father cuts him off and fires him, he won't be able to make a living. He hasn't worked anywhere except at his father's company, and it's all he knows how to do. If he gets fired from there, I'm scared he might do something...drastic."

I frowned again, wishing I had been here last night and maybe could've spotted that something was up with Jimmy. His father was one of my original card-playing customers from Charlottesville. He was also one of the biggest businessmen in Albemarle County.

"We're careful only to allow people to play who can afford their losses. But Jimmy's a legacy member; his father had to sign off on him and confirm that he had the wherewithal to cover any losses on his own."

"Yes, but at the time, his father didn't know about all the off-track gambling and online poker he's been involved in and that he had already lost almost everything. When he tells him that we can't afford to go on our honeymoon because he gambled away that money too, he'll go ballistic." She sobbed again.

Danny inhaled deeply, then sighed. "How much did he lose last night?"

"Twenty thousand dollars. The last bit of cash that he had. That we had."

I mulled this over in my head, then said, "Wait here, Miss Edwards." I went into my en suite bathroom and closed the door behind me. Stepping over to the sink, I grabbed the frame of the built-in medicine cabinet above it. After pressing a hidden catch, the unit swung away from the wall, exposing the front of a safe. I entered the combination and opened the door, then I withdrew a small brown paper bag and put four bundles of fifty-dollar bills wrapped with brown straps into it.

I closed the safe and returned the medicine cabinet to its original position. Then, I wrapped the open end of the bag tightly around the contents, creating a large, brown paper brick. Back in my office with my emotional visitor, I sat on the front edge of the guest chair next to hers and leaned over toward her.

I silently passed the bag with its contents over to Patti Edwards. When she looked inside, her eyes got wide. "I...I don't know what to say."

"I'm giving this to you on the condition that you'll tell Jimmy that I said he has to get help. I want him to enroll in Gambler's Anonymous today. I feel like I've failed him by not recognizing that he had a problem and not knowing that he could no longer withstand his own losses.

"Tell him that he's banned from gambling here permanently. In fact, I don't even want him showing his face in the dining room or bar until after he completes a full month at GA. Can you do that?"

She wiped both eyes with her fingers, looking at him gratefully. "Yes, I'll go straight to his office and tell him. Thank you, thank you so much; you don't know what this means to me...to us."

"Keep him busy, don't let him backslide. And have a wonderful honeymoon." I smiled at the young woman as we both stood up. I couldn't help it as my eyes stayed glued on her as she turned and left my office. *Jimmy is a lucky man*, I thought. He had someone who watched out for his best interests and was also an absolute fox. He could have a great life ahead if he got control of his gambling addiction. I figured it was probably three-to-one odds against that happening, but I hoped I was wrong.

THE YOUNG WOMAN, who called herself Patti Edwards, climbed into the back of the hired car that had been idling while waiting for her in the parking lot. Thankfully, the driver had kept the AC running, and it was doing a nice job of combatting central Virginia's midsummer heat. He pulled away from the club, slowly heading down the long, winding drive.

On the way, "Patti" removed the makeup she had deliberately applied pre-smeared. The dark circles and bags under her eyes had actually been pockets of dark eye shadow. Once it was removed, she quickly applied her normal makeup, not that she needed much since she was so naturally stunning. Then, after double-checking her phone to make certain that she had cell service this far out from Charlottesville, she dialed the memorized number.

"Vell?" The man with the Russian accent had picked up on the first ring, obviously expecting her call.

"It was easier than I thought it would be. He's incredibly sentimental and seems to have a need or desire to fix things. I think this could serve your purposes well."

The voice on the other end sounded amazed. "He gave you the full amount, yes?"

"Without batting an eye. His safe is somewhere in his office bathroom. As you know, he's young, in his early to mid-thirties. He might subconsciously feel guilty over his sudden success with the sportsman's club and the game." She paused momentarily, then said, "I hope this was what you were looking for."

"Of course it vas."

"Good. If you need anything else, I'll be happy to offer my services again."

"You ver helpful, and I vill keep that in mind. In addition to vat you were able to get from Reynolds, zere is bonus for you on ze plane. Von more ting, make sure you never go back to Crozet. Ve cannot afford to have you recognized by Reynolds again." With that, the man hung up.

CLIMBING aboard the small cabin Honda Jet, "Patti" found an envelope with another five thousand dollars on her seat. She smiled. The total payment wasn't out of line with other research and reconnaissance jobs she'd done for the man, but those had all been political targets on her home turf back in Washington, DC. This one had been very different but also very easy. She settled back into her seat as the pilot taxied out, preparing for takeoff and the short hop back to Dulles Airport.

~

A LITTLE AFTER 5:00 p.m....

"I DON'T FRIGGING BELIEVE IT." I was standing in the bar with Hitch, watching something that shouldn't be happening. Jimmy Hunter was walking into the bar with a couple of his friends. This was not three hours after I had given his fiancée those strict instructions to tell him he was at least temporarily barred from the premises.

Hitch looked at me curiously, followed my gaze across the room, and became just as dumbfounded as I was. "The kid has balls, Danny."

"Yeah, and I'm about to neuter his ass. How about asking him to join me in my office, Hitch? Don't embarrass him in front of his guests, but I need you to make him understand this isn't a request."

"Got it."

"HI, DANNY, WHAT'S UP?"

"What's up? Did your fiancée not make clear what I told her to tell you?"

"My what?"

"Fiancée. You know, that young blonde with legs so long that they should be continued on the next gal? Patti Edwards? The one you're marrying?"

"That's all news to me, Danny. I don't know any girl named Patti, and I'm sure as hell not getting married." He chuckled, thinking this was some kind of joke.

"Wait, you mean you didn't drop twenty g's in the game last night?"

"Drop twenty? Hell, no! I left eight grand ahead. Hey, are you okay? You look kind of sick."

I took a deep breath and forced a smile. "Nah, I'm good; somebody just played a trick on me."

"Looks like it wasn't all that funny."

"It wasn't. Hey, sorry to have disturbed your bar time. Tell the bartender to put a round of drinks for your group on my tab."

Jimmy looked confused but said, "Okay, and thanks. I hope you get back at whoever tricked you."

"Yeah, me too."

A minute after Jimmy left, Hitch came into the office. "He went back and sat down, then ordered a round of cocktails that he said was on you. I know I said he has balls, but that's taking things way too far."

I scowled. "He's not getting married. He didn't drop twenty last night; he was up eight. And he's got no idea who that girl was."

"What? But she knew all about him and the game! How the hell..."

I held up my hand. "I have no idea, but I'm sure as hell gonna find out and get my twenty grand back. And I'll make sure nothing like this ever happens again."

After Hitch returned to the club, I leaned back in my desk chair. I was a combination of angry, embarrassed, and humiliated over the Patti Edwards scam. I wasn't worried about Hitch saying anything; he knew all the details of all my businesses, even the illegal ones. He was completely capable of stepping in for me for short stints, which was why I could buy my boat and afford to spend time aboard it.

I had been the target of scammers before, but this was the only one who'd ever been successful. I briefly wondered if I might now be getting a little soft. However, I quickly dismissed the thought and then focused on creating a plan to find the woman and recover my twenty grand.

Recover. It struck me that this was the right word for what needed to happen. I needed a recovery expert. One who knew not only how to do the job but how to keep his mouth shut, and I knew where just the man for the job would be right now. I didn't need it getting around that I was a pushover, and this guy would make sure that didn't happen before others found out and decided to try taking their shots. I took out my phone and called Lana Jones, my brewpub manager.

"Hey, Lana, is Tripp Sanders there?"

"Yeah. You want to talk with him?"

"I do, but not over the phone. Ask him to come see me over at the club right away."

"Will do."

FIFTEEN MINUTES LATER, Tripp came into my office. I waved him into a chair. He must have been riding his Harley today since he was all decked out in leather and chains. Even without his biker gear, Tripp was an imposing person. About six feet tall, 240 pounds, with not an ounce of it fat, the guy was built like a giant fire hydrant. A scruffy beard with some gray streaks rounded out his tough look.

Tripp was also a professional airplane repossession agent. Chances are, if he showed up to confiscate your airplane, you might feel tempted to give him your keys and maybe some money for fuel. He was that kind of imposing. But right now, Tripp looked worried.

"Did that guy I sent you not work out last night?" He had recommended someone for a security position during the games.

"Hitch would know best; I wasn't here yesterday. But if your guy hadn't been good, you or I would've heard something about that from Hitch by now. That's not why I asked you to come up here." I then related the story of me getting fleeced; he didn't so much as blink. Tripp was one of the few trusted outsiders who knew about the games and advised me on security matters. He had been the one who had set up our camera system and vetted all our security guys who were on duty during the games.

"Any clue how she could have learned so much about your operation, Danny?"

"None, other than she knew a lot about the Hunters, too. Though Jimmy said he didn't know any woman named Patti."

"She wouldn't use her real name since she came here to rip you off."

I nodded. "Probably not."

Tripp scratched his chin through the beard. "I'll check the parking lot security camera recording and see if I can get a look at her car. One way or another, I'll find her, Danny."

OFFICE *of the Tidewater District Medical Examiner...*

SHERIFF "TINY" Clifford put a small dab of menthol salve under his nose before entering the autopsy room. The M.E. had forewarned him about both the smell and the body's condition, but it was even worse than he thought it would be. The menthol cut through some of the odor but not all of it.

Tiny demanded, "Show me."

"Like I said, Sheriff, it will all be in my final report, including any relevant pictures."

"If I wanted ta sit around an' wait ta read a goddamn report, I'd ah done that. I wanna see, an' I mean right now, so *show me!*"

The M.E. saw the murderous look on Tiny's face and quickly moved over to the autopsy table. Partially lifting the sheet covering the body, Tiny could see the skin of Billy's scalp had been pulled forward over his face, exposing the skull bone underneath. The M.E. removed the top half of the skull, which had been cut in such a way as to allow access to Billy's brain.

Tiny had been at enough autopsies over the years and had seen brains before, but none like this one. Billy's prolonged meth abuse had killed off sections of the lobes; those parts were withered and discolored. Crabs had eaten some of the back of his brain that had been exposed to the water where the skull had caved in, and what tissue was left there was badly damaged.

The M.E. began, "As you can see, the brain has deteriorated from prolonged substance abuse, probably methamphetamine. However, if you look here," he pointed to a bloody mass at the front of the brain. "You'll notice this hematoma, which was likely due to a whiplash-like effect from a coup-contrecoup injury where the brain bounced back and forth within the skull. I say likely because the back part of the brain is missing, so I can't examine it.

"The exact cause of death was blunt force trauma to the back of the skull," he picked up the top of the skull, which showed the damage at the rear. "See these marks? Whatever weapon did this was long and had a blunt edge, about three-eighths of an inch thick."

Tiny's brow furrowed. "What, like an axe?"

"Not unless it hadn't been sharpened in a hundred years. No, the leading edge was completely flat."

"So, that whiplash thing, it happened when he died?"

"No, it likely happened at least several hours before. It would take a while for a clot that size to form. His heart stopped beating the second his skull caved in. Even though bruising can still happen from the blood that's already in the circulatory system, this wouldn't have had time to create this large of a clot; it was from a slow, continuous bleed. Also, I found several old and new bruises and scrapes on his knuckles, probably from different fights at various times. There was one very curious horizontal injury across his back, just above his waist. It looked like he was hit with a round bar or a pipe or a very thin bat."

"That happened when he was killed?"

"Probably. It's likely that it had to do with that same fight."

"Back ta that whiplash thing. Would this slow his reflexes, maybe make him more of an easy target for gettin' jumped?"

The M.E. looked thoughtful, "I can't say for certain, but it's possible."

"Yeah, well, you just make sure an' talk that part up in your report. I think I just got me ah prime suspect."

BRANDY LOOKED up from behind the bar as two sheriff's cars pulled up at the base of the dock. Tiny and two deputies raced past the restaurant and disappeared into the covered dock section. They reemerged five minutes later, and the sheriff made a beeline for the bar.

"Hey, girl, you see that Jeep hot-rod boy today? He ain't on Jay Martin's old boat, the one he was supposed to buy."

"Early this morning, but he left a while ago, Sheriff."

"He say when he was comin' back?"

"Next week, I think."

"Any idea where he went?" The sheriff leaned over the bar, causing Brandy to back away from him as flashes of their previous encounter entered her mind.

"I think he said he was going home."

"He say where that was?"

"Somewhere over by one of the mountains."

"There's a lot of damn mountains in Virginia, girl! Which one are we talkin' about?"

"I'm not sure."

From his office, Cam had noticed the sheriff on the security cameras. He now walked up next to him. "Something I can do for you, Sheriff?"

"Yeah, you were next on my list. I need the originals and any copies that ya got of your security video that shows that Jeep guy fighting' my cousin. My now *dead* cousin."

Cam hadn't heard the news about Billy, and Brandy was doing a good imitation of being shocked as if she had just learned this. Even though he truly didn't feel this way, Cam said, "I'm sorry for your loss, Sheriff."

"I'll bet, especially since you wanted ta kick him outta here. Now, how about gettin' those tapes?"

"I don't have any tapes, exactly. It's all stored in real-time on the cloud, meaning it's all at a server farm somewhere in the Midwest. I can download and send you a copy, though."

"Yeah, do that." The sheriff was thrown off by this development. He'd wanted to be able to "lose" any video evidence that showed his cousin as an aggressor who had come out swinging, completely unprovoked. Now, if some defense attorney got ahold of it, they could use it to show that Billy was a bully with a temper, which was exactly what Tiny was trying to avoid happening. This development wasn't good news.

The sheriff took out two business cards, handing one to Cam and another to Brandy. "You two see that boy in the Jeep show up, an' you call me straightaway. I gotta lot of questions I want ta ask him. What's his last name, anyhow? I know you called him Danny the other day. You got his home address?"

Cam smiled. "His name is Danny Reynolds. He took over Jay's dockage contract, and we haven't updated it with his information yet. But he'll be back here on Tuesday afternoon."

"Oh yeah? You sure about that?"

"Yes, that's when we're closing on our deal. He's buying half of my business and property, and we're paying off that note. You can tell Ted to expect us to drop off a check then."

First, the color drained from Tiny's face, then red began seeping back in as he realized the deal he'd been counting on and desperately needing was about to blow up in his face. "Who is this guy, Reynolds, anyway?"

Seeing Tiny get so shaken up gave Brandy some newfound courage. "He's someone that can make one phone call and get the two million to pay off you and Ted. He's got a lot of friends in DC that you guys won't want anything to do with. Powerful friends with a lot of clout."

Tiny didn't like this brave new side of her. "You sure seem ta know a lot about him, girl."

Brandy smiled smugly, another first for her when she was around Tiny. "Probably more than you would ever want to know."

BACK IN THE privacy of his cruiser, Tiny called Ted, relating what he'd just heard about the marina property.

"Who is this asshole? He can't do that, not when we have Cam Thomas right where we want him with his back against the wall! I'm not letting anyone screw this up, and you damn sure better not, either. You're supposed to take care of stuff like this; that's your part of the deal, Tiny."

"His name's Danny Reynolds. He's supposed ta have a lotta big dick buddies up in DC. But there's more." Tiny told him about the autopsy findings and the bar fight.

"Is there anything you can hold him on?"

"Mebbe manslaughter if we stretch it a bit. But a judge might grant him bail."

"You let me worry about what the judge does; you just arrest this Reynolds before he can close that deal with Thomas. Where's he live?"

"Somewhere way over in the mountains. But don't worry, since he's comin' back on Tuesday, I'll be waitin' for his ass when he shows up."

5

THE ART OF RELAXATION

I saw it was Cam on my phone. "Hey, Cam."

"Hey, Danny. I need to give you a heads-up; Tiny was here looking for you."

"What did he want?"

"I'm not sure, but it had something to do with that scuffle you had with Billy. Tiny wanted any and all video recordings of it, and I got the idea that he wanted to make that all disappear. It turns out that Billy's dead, and I think Tiny might somehow be trying to pin his death on you."

My mind was now racing. As far as I knew, that video would show that I'd been attacked. It would also show Billy leaving under his own power. "He walked off just fine afterward. Besides, he started it! There's nothing there to 'pin' on me."

"Which is why I think he was looking to make that video evidence all go away so that he can frame you. But this also tells me they think that Billy had help exiting this life."

I quickly said, "I've only been around there for a grand total of a few days, and I've already heard that there were a lot of people willing to stand in line for a chance to help out with that."

"Yeah, there were." Cam took a deep breath and said, "But that's not all, Danny, I screwed up and let Tiny catch me off guard. I told him about us throwing in together and planning on paying off the note. I told him that we'd drop in on Ted this Tuesday afternoon. I'm sorry about that, but I couldn't get the picture out of my mind of his smug face when he handed me that notice. I'm usually smarter than to let my feelings drive my actions."

Damn. I'd wanted to spring it on those two without any advanced warning, though I couldn't blame Cam for telling Tiny. There was indeed something so infuriating about how the sheriff had leered at Cam as he'd handed him that notice calling his note. Tiny had enjoyed it, and coupled with his usual rotten demeanor, it's not surprising that Cam wanted to hit him back.

"Don't worry about it; they were going to find out soon enough anyway. I just wish I'd been there to see his face."

"Yeah, paybacks are a bitch. But I'm worried that he might try and waylay you when you get here."

"That thought crossed my mind, too. This is why I need you to come over here Sunday night so we can take care of the paperwork at my lawyer's office in Charlottesville first thing Monday morning. We can't trust any of the lawyers down there not to have some Clifford connections."

"That's a good idea."

I added, "We can have dinner here at the sportsman's club on Sunday night, and you can stay in one of the member guest rooms. After we do all the paperwork in the morning, we'll drive straight to Mathews and hand Ted Clifford a certified check around noon. We'll still catch him off guard, and once he has been paid off, he'll have missed his chance to try to pull some crap using Tiny to try and stop us."

"That sounds great." I could tell by his voice that he was relieved that I wasn't angry over his slip of the tongue and that he was happy to do whatever was needed to fix things. "Oh, and Brandy asked me to tell you that she'll give you a call when she gets back to her houseboat after work but that it might be kind of late."

I chuckled, "What might be late to someone with a nine-to-five job doesn't apply to me since I keep similar hours to hers, so that'll be fine. And I'll text you the club's address for your GPS."

"Sounds good. I'll see you Sunday night."

~

I WAS HALFWAY EXPECTING Parker to show up with her father so she could try to control our conversation, but Alex came by himself. From my office, I saw his Maserati coming up the drive on one of the security camera feeds, so I went to the garage to meet him. As he stepped out of the car, he looked around and smiled.

"You know, Danny, I always liked this setup, but I like it even more now that I'm going to own part of it. I'm glad that you picked me as your partner. I'm also glad that whatever happened with Parker this morning hasn't changed that. I tried asking her about it, but she kept changing the subject, so I never did get to the bottom of it, though I knew it couldn't have been good."

I reached out and shook his hand. "Like I told you earlier, if I had needed you to intervene, you wouldn't have wanted me as a partner. And I never for a second considered anyone else, Alex. I'm glad to have you on board."

I had Hitch set us up in the small private dining room that I used for business, which set off to the side of the main one. As we walked through the regular dining room, I was glad to see that we were quite busy. I saw Alex scanning the main room, obviously taking in the numbers. He nodded and smiled at a few members, who had looked up and acknowledged him as he did. He was popular with most of the other members, not just the secret card game players.

After we'd settled in at our table with the door closed, Alex commented, "That's a pretty good crowd out there, Danny, some real hitters in it, too." He paused for a moment, then said, "Do you want to know why I didn't push you for a controlling interest? It's because, first, I knew you wouldn't go for it, and second, I'm so damn impressed with what you've accomplished with this place in such a relatively short amount of time. I know I don't need to spend my time trying to direct things since you can handle it all, and hopefully, that includes my daughter. Though I'm afraid that she might turn out to be the most difficult part of our deal."

"Thanks, Alex. You're right; I'd have never given up more than forty-nine percent. And yes, Parker does like to jump in and take over, but you already knew that about her. I think if she can learn to listen and observe before dipping her oars into things, she might become a great asset to you at some point in the future. I know she's very interested in the club's business, and there's a lot she can learn here if she's just willing to watch and observe first."

"I take it she wasn't doing that earlier."

"As I said, if she can learn a bit more restraint and a little more focus, she could be quite an asset to you. Maybe even to both of us."

"I haven't had much luck teaching her those things."

"You're her father, the only parent in her life, and you love her. You have a hard time telling her no, and I get that. But I don't have those things holding me back."

If it had been anyone else who was more than twenty years older than me, I don't think I'd have spoken so freely about their daughter. Because I felt comfortable doing so, this reinforced the feeling that Alex and I should have a good relationship going forward. I call 'em like I see 'em.

"So, you're willing to mentor to her, Danny?"

"I don't know that I'd call it that, but I know she's going to want to be around here more, so she might as well learn a few things while she is."

"First of all, thank you. And secondly, good luck with that." He chuckled. While he loved and overly spoiled his daughter, he had no misconceptions about how she really acted.

At this point, Hitch brought in our drinks. As the manager, he wasn't a regular server. However, he knew that this being our first partner meeting, we'd want as much privacy as possible. With Hitch being my most trusted associate, I was comfortable talking in front of him.

Alex said, "Hello, Hitch. It's good to see you. And Danny, this is another reason that I wanted to be in this place with you. We never ordered drinks, yet here are our usual cocktails. This is the type of attention to detail that makes this place so special."

Hitch beamed. "Hello, Mr. Phipps. Thank you. We try to do our best."

After taking a sip, Alex said, "You succeeded. Do we need menus?"

Hitch replied, "We have your favorite tonight, sautéed jumbo Virginia sea scallops with a house-grown vegetable medley."

"Like I said, attention to detail." Alex smiled broadly. "That sounds great, I'll take it."

I said, "Make that two."

As Hitch left, Alex said, "He was quite a find."

"He was on the construction crew I originally hired to refurbish this part of the property. I liked him because he was so sharp; way too sharp to be stuck doing what he had been doing. When I hired him for the club, he hit the ground running and never looked back."

"You were quite a find as well. You're the first guy Parker likes that I approve of."

"Alex, there's nothing between Parker and me, and there won't ever be."

"Oh, I know that. The question is whether or not my daughter does." He laughed loudly while I cringed inside. After he took another sip of his drink, he asked, "So, what is it that you're interested in enough to sell off part of the club? And why the big hurry?"

I related the story about Mobjack Creek Marina, leaving out just the part about me killing Billy Clifford. I also selectively edited the part that included Brandy.

"Why are you deliberately kicking a hornet's nest? It sounds like that sheriff has it in for you."

"By the time I get through, even his dog will hate me. But there's something about the place. The first time I saw it, I had the same feeling I got when I initially saw this property. Sometimes, you have to go with your gut. And I don't like it when some jerk thinks he's such hot stuff that he can order anyone else around, especially when it's me. Plus, I hate developers like Ted Clifford. It reminds me of how they've ruined Crozet. And can you imagine the size of the balls it takes to show a property to investors when you don't even own it yet?"

"That was crass, for certain. But I totally get the part about you wanting to own part of that place; it's just like me and this club. It's not enough to be a member; I want to be part of it."

"Exactly. We're both of the same mindset."

OUR CONVERSATION over dinner became less about business and more about Alex wanting to get to know me more on a personal level. I mean, we *knew* each other, but in a more formal way in my position as a club owner and his as an important customer/member. What I didn't know but learned through this conversation was that Alex had a dossier on me that had been put together by a crack investigative team. He had it assembled when he first joined the club and started to play in the poker games. He wanted to be assured that the games weren't fixed. From his operatives, he learned that I was no cheater and that, in fact, I had already permanently banned one player who I discovered was marking cards during play. That word had gotten around, which was part of why my games became so popular with big-hitter players. They knew we were watching and wouldn't put up with that kind of crap.

By the time we finished dessert, both Alex and I were reassured that we'd made the right choices. We moved outside onto the dining room's private loggia area. It faced south and had an incredible view, looking down the Blue Ridge mountain range. About fifteen feet from the edge of its tiled floor was a ten-foot-wide creek that was running fast, giving off a relaxing sound as it passed, splashing across the rocks on its way down the mountain.

From a cigar caddy in my pocket, I produced a pair of Connecticut tobacco cigars that we both lit before leaning back in our padded patio chairs.

"There's something about this place, Danny. Owning part of it, I mean. I sat out here once before with you, but this time, it has an entirely different feel to me."

I nodded. "I remember the first time I sat out here and the feeling that hit me when I did. It was relaxing, listening to the water, but I knew I had to make this place a success if I was going to be able to keep enjoying it. The weight of that reality was huge." I took another puff of my cigar as I glanced over at Alex, who was now the perfect picture of relaxation.

"Don't get me wrong; I love our vineyard property, Danny, but this place has a completely different feel. Maybe it's because I have that same weight of responsibility at the vineyards that you were talking about. But here, I know that I can just enjoy it without having to share the burden of running it. You and Hitch have things well in hand, and all I have to do is relax and enjoy what the club has to offer, including my cut of the cash." He grinned.

"That's exactly how I feel about my marina. I don't want to run it; I only want to enjoy it. That, and ruin Ted Clifford's day." It was my turn to smile.

"Danny, I think this is the start of a beautiful partnership."

"I couldn't agree more, Alex. I couldn't agree more."

Two hours later, in Danny's bedroom:

After having let herself into Danny's unlocked apartment, Parker then knocked lightly on the bedroom door. Hearing no reply, she quietly opened the door and slipped into the empty room. That's when she heard the shower running in the en suite bath. Smiling to herself, she briefly thought about sneaking in and surprising Danny by joining him.

Then, a different plan took root in her mind, and she quickly stripped down and stretched naked across his bed. She thought that while he was the only man who had ever turned her down, there was no way that he would do that again with her being both naked and eager right here in his own bed. Suddenly, his phone began to vibrate on the nightstand. Picking it up, she saw that it was a video call from some chick named Brandy, and a pang of jealousy shot through her. She'd never heard Danny mention anyone by that name before. The contact picture showed a pretty blond woman with a nice smile and deep blue eyes.

Parker tapped the answer button and held the camera far enough away to also include her naked breasts, Danny's pillows, and the bed's headboard. "Hello?"

Brandy was taken aback at the image she saw. "I'm sorry, I've got the wrong number. I was trying to reach Danny Reynolds."

"Oh, you've got the right number, all right, but Danny's in the shower right now and can't come to the phone."

"Who the hell are you?" Brandy demanded.

"I could ask you the same thing, bitch. Why are you calling my boyfriend?"

Brandy hesitated, then said, "I'm also starting to wonder why." After another pause, she asked, "You wouldn't happen to be Parker, would you?"

Parker smiled cruelly. "Oh, he told you about me, did he? That's funny; in all the time we've been together, he's never once mentioned you. I guess the cheating sex must not have been that great. Do yourself a favor, and don't call back. We won't want any interruptions." She squinted, her eyes matching her faux smile as she hit the "end" button.

Aboard her houseboat in Mobjack Creek, Brandy was now feeling a combination of anger and humiliation. Danny had told her that Parker "wasn't his type" and that he'd always turned her down and didn't want to date her. He also said that she was "drop-dead gorgeous," and from what she'd just seen—and she'd seen a lot more than she bargained for—this was an accurate statement. Apparently, the son of a bitch had been lying about everything else.

Suddenly, it hit her: not only had Danny fooled her and rushed her into bed, but now he was about to become her boss and landlord. Not only that, but they shared the same finger pier to access their boats. Even worse, he knew her deepest secret about what had happened on that dark road two years ago. Though she knew all about Danny killing Billy, which was *his* deepest, darkest secret. At least, she thought it was up until now, though she wasn't sure what to believe anymore.

He had seemed to her like one of the really good guys, and she'd even allowed herself to think that there might eventually be more to their relationship, like maybe having it turn into a real one instead of a one-night stand—or rather, a two-night stand. Obviously, now, there was no way. He'd apparently led her on while already in a relationship with another woman back in his hometown. She felt used, and was angry about having to live next door to him, at least part-time. The only thing that didn't fit in all of this was the fact that he'd come to her rescue when Billy attacked her. If he was really such a jerk, why would he have done this?

Suddenly, her phone rang, the specific tone indicating it was a video call. She saw Danny's face on the screen and pressed "Decline," setting the phone down. Seconds later, the normal audio call tone sounded. Seeing his face again on her phone, she also pressed Decline. A minute after that, the text tone sounded. For a split second, she considered reading it but then decided not to, at least not now. There was no way for him to lie his way out of what she'd seen with her own two eyes: a naked woman waiting for him in what she assumed was his bed while he was taking a shower.

Brandy knew that talking to him right now would be a mistake; she was far too angry and humiliated and would undoubtedly say some things she might regret later. No, she needed a shower and a good night's sleep before confronting him. The shower was key to sorting out the thoughts in her head, and sleep would be her only escape from how she was feeling now. Not that she expected it would be a particularly restful night.

∽

I GUESS I shouldn't have been as shocked as I was at the sight that greeted me when I came out of my bathroom. I mean, after knowing her for a couple of years, you'd have thought I'd have learned by now that Parker would stop at nothing to get what she wanted.

"What the hell, Parker? Get your clothes on and get out of my apartment!"

"Gee, Danny, after all the trouble I went to in dressing for the occasion! I see you got my note about what to wear tonight."

Damn, that woman had such an evil smirk. That's when it hit me: she wasn't the only naked person in the room. It was how I slept, and I hadn't been expecting company.

"I mean it, Parker, get the hell out!"

"I hear your big head telling me to get out, but I see your little head disagrees with the idea."

Parker pointed to my nether region, where something had apparently begun forming its own decision about the proper course of action for this evening. I thought about retreating to my bathroom to collect a towel to wrap around my waist. But instead, I went over to my dresser, where I put on a pair of boxers. I was trying to make it seem like this had been my plan all along. I didn't want to encourage Parker by looking weak or possibly having any intention of giving in.

I turned back to the bed and said, "I'm not kidding, Parker. You need to put on your clothes and leave. And you'd better not break in here again."

"I didn't 'break in,' Danny; you left the doors unlocked between here and the garage. Anyone with a door clicker could've walked in like I did. And I read that agreement you and my father signed. I'm just exercising the clause about allowing us an 'unannounced inspection of the premises.' And I'm offering you a similar clause." She slid one foot back, raising that knee while, uh, expanding the view of her own nether region.

"If you had read the whole agreement, you'd have seen that it specifically excludes my office and apartment in what can be inspected without notice. And don't you think that you've already pulled enough crap around here for one day? Now, get out; I'm expecting a call. A *private* call."

"If you're talking about that Brandy chick, she already called. We had a lovely chat."

"What do you mean by that?"

"Oh, nothing...I just explained that you and I have a lot of history together. Come to think of it, she might have taken that part the wrong way..."

I grabbed the cocktail dress she had draped across the back of a chair. That was all I found; there were no panties or bra along with it, which didn't come as a real surprise. I wadded it up and threw the dress at her. Subtlety didn't work with Parker. "Put that on and get out of here!"

"Hey! Be careful with that; it's a one-of-a-kind Stella McCartney! Her father was a Beatle!" She started smoothing the material.

"I couldn't care less about whose it is. Wait, you told Brandy *what*?"

"I wanted her to know that you and I have been...friends...for a long time."

I grabbed my phone and saw that Brandy had indeed called, and it had been a *video* call. Knowing Parker, she undoubtedly would've ensured that Brandy got an eyeful. Now, I snatched the dress back out of Parker's hands, wadded it up again in a tight ball, then opened my door and tossed it into the living room of my apartment. Parker shrieked.

"Damn you, Danny, I told you that was a..."

I interrupted her, "Yeah, I know. It's a Ringo Starr. Now, go put it on and get out of here before I throw it in the dumpster." She leaped off my bed and chased after that obviously overpriced potato sack. As soon as she was through the bedroom door, I slammed and locked it behind her. It wasn't the only door I'd be locking from now on.

I went over and sat on the edge of my bed and hit "Redial" on the video phone app. Instead of seeing Brandy's face, I got a message that the person I was calling wasn't accepting video calls at present. So, I tried a regular audio call, but it went to voicemail in two rings instead of the usual four. Brandy had manually declined the call. Then I texted her, asking for a chance to explain. It showed "Delivered" but not "Read." *Damn you, Parker!*

BRANDY WAS AWAKENED at 2:30 a.m. by a strange thumping sound. Like most liveaboards on boats, she had become attuned to sounds other than the faint underwater clicks, those usual marine life sounds, and squeaks from the mooring lines. Ignoring any *un*usual sounds meant taking the chance of waking up and getting your feet wet—hopefully, only your feet. And this repeated thumping sound was definitely not usual.

The thumping continued to repeat itself, this time accompanied by a muffled voice. She fought through the fog of sleep and realized it was someone at her door. Slipping into her robe, she went through the salon and turned on her deck light before opening the door. A very weary-looking Danny with a deeply concerned face looked back at her.

6

BACK AGAIN

I was looking into the face of one very pissed-off lady.

"Damn it, Danny, I was asleep. Do you have any idea what time it is?"

I nodded. "Trust me, I'm well aware. But since you wouldn't take my calls or read my texts, you left me no choice but to drive over here and explain what happened..."

She put her hand up, palm out, stopping me mid-sentence.

"When someone declines your calls and texts, it means they don't want to talk to you. At least, not right then. So, take the hint and go the hell away."

I shook my head, "No! Not until after you've heard what I've come to say. The least you can do is let me explain what happened. Then, if you still don't want to talk to me, I'll leave."

"The least I can do? Are you kidding me? You've got a lot of gall; either that or you think I'm a special kind of stupid. I know what happened, Danny, I've got eyes. Before we went to dinner, I had asked you straight up if you were married or involved, and what I saw on the video call looked very involved, unless you run a nudist camp. Wait, you know what? You've had over three hours to come up with undoubtedly the biggest cock-and-bull story in history, so yeah, take your best shot and explain. This ought to be good."

"Can I at least come in and tell you in private? Sound travels far over the water, you know, especially when it's this calm."

"I think most everyone around here is probably asleep...you know...like I was." She frowned, then seemed to think it over. Then, reluctantly, she stepped back and waved me inside, leaving plenty of room for me to pass by. She took a seat in the single chair across from the couch, ensuring that I wouldn't be sitting near her. I settled on the couch and began to recount the afternoon, starting with how Parker had started pushing her weight around with the club staff and telling members that she was the new owner.

I went into as much detail as possible because, if you're selling a lie, you wouldn't normally give such in-depth information. It leaves too many points exposed that could be argued if they were false. I told her about my dinner with Alex and then finally about going back to my apartment after the club closed for the night. I watched her face the whole time and thought it might have softened slightly as I talked. Maybe. Hopefully.

"You expect me to believe all that?"

"It's the truth, so, yes."

She stared silently at me for a minute, then said, "It's Paul McCartney's daughter that's the designer, not Ringo Starr's."

I shrugged because I seriously had no clue and didn't care. I was a little surprised that she knew since she didn't seem to be interested in designer clothes and seemed to be more into casual wear. As if reading my mind, she said, "Just because I can't afford to wear her stuff doesn't mean I don't know who she is. And even if I could afford it, that's not my style."

I took the fact that we were talking about a relatively small and, to me, an insignificant part of what I told her to be a good sign. Rather than focus on something else, I thought I'd work with this, finding that common ground. "I figured it was expensive."

"One of her off-the-rack dresses costs more than I make in a month."

Okay, maybe this wasn't such a good idea after all. "Oh."

"That wasn't a shot about what I get paid. I make more here than I could at most of the other bars in the area. It just fits with what I would expect your little girlfriend to wear."

"Again, she's not my girlfriend! What do I have to do to convince you of that? She's just the pain-in-the-ass daughter of my now new partner."

She gave me a sly smile. "You don't have to do anything; I believe you. Even if she was your girlfriend, kicking her naked ass out of your bed so you could drive all the way over here would've ended that." She paused then said, "I have to admit, from what I saw of her, and I saw a *lot*, I'm pretty flattered that you did that. Or, rather, that you didn't do *her*." She chuckled.

"Like I told you, she's not even close to being my type."

"And I am?"

I shrugged my shoulders slightly. "I'm sitting here, aren't I? And aren't we supposed to go out again on my next trip over here?"

"Is this visit because I'm your type or because I'm the sole witness to you killing Billy Clifford, and you don't want me to call Crime Stoppers because I'm pissed at you?"

I hesitated to answer. Not because I was afraid of the answer but because the question had been framed in such a way that if I responded to the part about killing Billy, if this boat was bugged, I could be handing a prosecutor a gift-wrapped confession. I let my eyes dart around the room as I said, "You said that Tiny was snooping around, looking for me." This was the first time I'd sidestepped a question from her, a fact that wasn't lost on her as she watched me look around.

"Yes, I did. So what, you think I'm working for him now? Or do you not want to answer the first part of the question?"

"I have no problem answering the first part of that question. Yeah, you are my type, and I'd like to keep seeing you. I thought I'd made that part pretty clear before, but there you go, now I've spelled it out."

"For the record, I don't and won't have anything to do with Tiny."

"I know you wouldn't. But you can't be too careful about wiretaps and bugs, especially with such a slimeball like Tiny."

"'Careful,' says the man running around in a rare Jeep that sticks out like a sore thumb."

"I drove over tonight in an SUV the club owns, just in case. There aren't many vehicles on the road this late, and you're right; the Jeep would be easy to spot."

"You took a heck of a risk coming back tonight."

"It would have been a bigger risk not to. I couldn't leave things the way they were between us and have you thinking I was a liar."

"I'm glad. But I would have eventually talked to you after I had a good night's sleep and cooled off."

That was good to know. I filed that fact away in my brain, then replied, "I wasn't sure."

"You are now." She gave me a warm smile, followed by a big yawn.

The yawn proved contagious, with me joining in. "Looks like we're both exhausted. Sorry to wake you up, but I'm glad we got things sorted out. I'm going to go over to my boat and crash for what's left of the night, grab some breakfast at the restaurant in the morning, and head back."

"Not a good idea, Danny. Tiny might have his marine patrol keeping an eye on your boat. Seeing any lights on in it would be a dead giveaway. And until you and Cam pay off the Clifford note, it would probably be a good idea for you to avoid being seen at the restaurant. Now that he knows you are about to wreck their plan, he'll want to put you in jail, at least until they can foreclose. He left his card with me and Cam, telling us to call if we saw you around. So, stay here tonight, and I'll fix us breakfast in the morning."

I nodded. "All I'm probably good for tonight is sleep. Unlike you, I haven't had any of it yet."

"I didn't get much sleep since I was so upset. But we can still see what else you're good for." She stood up and held out a hand, then pulled me up off the couch and led me back to her bedroom.

. . .

EVEN THOUGH THE houseboat was under the shed roof part of the docks, the morning sun made a direct hit for an hour or so right after sunrise. The window curtains were sheer enough to allow some of that light into the room. As I slowly became aware of my surroundings, I saw the other side of Brandy's queen-sized bed was empty, and some great breakfast smells were making their way into the room. I got dressed in the same clothes I'd arrived in, then went into the en suite head.

When I emerged from her bedroom, Brandy looked up from the stove and smiled. "Good morning, sunshine! How'd you sleep?"

"Like the dead after you wore me out. How about you?"

"Pretty much the same. There's coffee ready." She motioned to a coffeemaker on the counter.

I bypassed the coffeemaker long enough to hug her from behind. "Thanks for listening and believing."

"Thanks for not blaming me for jumping to conclusions and for schlepping all the way over here to clear things up. That Parker chick is a piece of...work."

I released her and then filled a mug she'd left out on the counter for me. "You don't know the half of it. She was a special kind of pissed off when I threw her out." I laughed, remembering what happened.

"From what I saw on the video call, she's stunning. I bet that's the first time anyone ever kicked her out of bed." She glanced over, probably looking for my reaction. When I chuckled, she seemed satisfied and went back to concentrating on what she was cooking.

"Probably. But her beauty is only skin deep, and the bullcrap that comes with it is way too much to contend with. She's got a lot of growing up to do, and that won't happen unless Alex quits coddling her. Life has yet to kick her in the ass, but it will at some point, and it's going to be ugly when it does."

"It sounds like you already taught her a couple of life lessons yesterday," Brandy said as she handed me a hot breakfast burrito.

"We'll at least call it a good start on a life lesson."

"You told Alex you'd be willing to teach her about your business?"

The way she said it sounded like there were a few implied questions hidden within that statement. I replied, "If I didn't know better, I'd say you sound worried. Don't be."

"Hey, you're a big boy and free to do what you want and even who you want."

This sounded about as insincere as it gets. I said, "I do, and I did. That's why I came here last night; I prefer your company."

"That feeling is mutual, Danny. I've already said I'd like to spend more time with you."

"Good, because I was already planning on it. We can start as soon as Cam and I get things settled on Monday."

I LEFT RIGHT AFTER BREAKFAST, walking alone up the dock and over to the parking area. We'd agreed that I should have a few minutes head start so we wouldn't be spotted together. I didn't want Tiny to get word that Brandy had seen me but hadn't alerted him.

I had just climbed into the white Cadillac Escalade I'd driven over last night when I spotted a sheriff's car pulling into the parking area. Fortunately, this SUV had limo tint on the rear passenger windows and the darkest tint allowed by law on the driver and passenger windows. I wasn't likely to be spotted unless whoever was in that car looked straight into the SUV through the front windshield, which was currently turned away from them.

Still, I slid down as far as I could in the seat and made sure not to tap the brake pedal accidentally. Even though I hadn't started the car yet, the brake lights would still work. Fortunately, it being the start of the weekend, there were more cars parked in the lot this morning. I realized I was holding my breath after the cruiser pulled past me and stopped in an empty handicap parking space.

From my vantage point in the darkened interior of the car, I watched as Tiny got out and made his way down the dock, pausing to look in the windows of the closed dockside bar before continuing on. After he disappeared into the covered shed area, I started the SUV and slowly made my way over toward the start of the asphalt road. Then I kept my speed right at the legal limit through the county, knowing that Tiny and his deputies loved handing out tickets. I was extra cautious until I got out of his jurisdiction.

I waited until I was past West Point before calling Brandy. "Hey, how's everything going?"

She said, "I had a friend drop by here. He came into the bar on his way out. He had been checking on that boat he'd been watching."

We were being careful not to speak too openly. To anyone else, it might have sounded like she was talking about Billy's boat, but instead, she was talking about mine. "Gotcha. Glad it hasn't sunk on him."

"Me too. By the way, I'm looking forward to seeing you again when you come over on Tuesday."

"Right back at you on that." My phone started vibrating, and I saw a call coming in from Tripp Sanders, my plane repo guy. "Oops, I've got a business call; I've got to go."

"Ah. The Ferrari princess strikes again," she teased.

"Definitely not her. I'll call you later."

With that, I switched lines. "Tell me something good, Tripp."

"I'll tell you something weird, Danny. Your pal Patti used a hired car from the airport to the club and straight back. She arrived and departed by a chartered Honda jet. Both rides were paid for by a credit card with a Cayman Islands billing address. It's managed by a law firm down there—a very large firm with some big US connections, a few in DC. Which is not all that strange since the jet originated from and returned to Dulles. A black Suburban picked her up there, but the camera angle wasn't good enough to get a plate number."

"A black Suburban in DC...there are probably more of those up there than the total number of cars in Crozet."

"Exactly. So we've reached a dead end. Sorry that I couldn't find out more."

"Actually, you might have found out enough, Tripp. Thanks for the quick work."

"Hey, I hope it helps."

After he hung up, this new information began spinning around in my head. Someone had decided to probe my business's security, and I had failed the test. This had to have been someone familiar with the major players in Charlottesville in order to be aware of the Hunter family. They also knew about the games and that Jimmy Hunter participated in them. And they had a DC connection since that's where the girl came from. Obviously, she was a pro of some type; DC is full of hustlers and hookers. Some of them aren't even in elected offices.

So, who in DC might benefit from doing this? Assuming someone was behind "Patti," and she was hired to do the job, there were much cheaper ways to approach it. The jet time alone would've cost a quarter of what she stole, and the club was only a couple-hour drive from DC. Private jets were tools used by people whose time was far too valuable to spend any behind the wheel of a car on a road with us mere mortals. This was another reason I thought the woman was a hired pro. But hired by whom? And an even bigger question was *why?*

The first name that came to my mind was Alex. As a new partner, he might want to be sure of how I would handle the situation and whether or not I'd learned anything from it. But he didn't bring it up last night, which I'd have done if I were him. So, I just wasn't sure. But it wasn't like I lacked other suspects. More than a couple of dozen card players from DC belonged to the club, though I couldn't think of any who would risk losing their ability to play over twenty grand. Unless it was some secret thrill by a closeted crazy person. You never knew how some people got their kicks.

So, we were stuck in a blind alley at this point, with Tripp having run out of clues. And he was the best. If he couldn't find anything more, it was doubtful anyone else could, either. But he had given me enough information to give me a direction to watch. I say "watch" because this might not be a one-time thing. Not that I thought they were stupid enough to try the same thing twice, and as I said, I didn't think this was just about money. Though the Cayman Island angle did smell like big money. The kind that wouldn't get their hands dirty over a paltry (to them) twenty grand. So, unless the person behind this stunt learned all they wanted or got enough kicks this time, chances were we hadn't heard the last from them.

While there was nothing quite so unnerving as waiting for the other shoe to drop, I had a lot of work to do at my brewery. This would keep me busy if I was going to take my moonshine business legit. At the very least, it would take my mind off the scammer and the scam. I would drop off the Escalade at the club, pick up my Jeep, and head to Moonrise Brewery. While my morning was shot, there was still a lot of daylight left and plenty of work still ahead to cram into it.

7

THE TOURIST TRAIN

I spent the rest of the day at Moonrise, working out a plan with my distiller, Luke, that would take us out of the shadows and onto the liquor store shelves. In addition to making first-class moonshine, Luke was also an expert on liquor laws, even though he didn't abide by them, at least not yet. We finished a little before five, and I grabbed a lager, taking it out on the side loading dock for some fresh air. The dock's platform faced the train tracks, which were about twenty-five feet away from where I was standing. I heard an engine coming, and it tooted its horn about a half mile down the tracks.

This was near where a developmentally challenged young African-American man lived. He was in one of the small houses across from the tracks, and he loved the trains. Rain or shine, he came out of his house and stood on the sidewalk, waving wildly until the last car passed, completely lost in the excitement of that passing train. Sometimes, it was an empty coal train headed back to West Virginia to get reloaded before being taken down to Norfolk to be put on freighters for export. Other times, it was one of the two Amtrak trains that traveled between DC and Chicago each day. They usually passed each other in or near Crozet in the afternoons, heading in opposite directions. But in this case, it was just our local tourist train.

Seeing the trains coming through was a great part of our small-town way of life.

The engineers of most of the trains that came through our town recognized this young man. They tooted their horns as they passed his house, bringing a lot of joy into his life. Could you imagine this happening in Miami or Philadelphia? Me neither; it was a great perk of living in small-town America.

The family that owned our local short-line railroad had bought a few vintage passenger cars for their private collection and had been renovating them over the past few years. A couple of years ago, they decided to share part of their collection with the public by creating the little tourist train. It consisted of two vintage, restored dining cars pulled behind an older engine. Thursday through Sunday, it left from over the mountain in Staunton (pronounced Stan-ton—call it Stawn-ton, and we locals will know instantly you're not from around here) in the morning for a three-hour run back and forth to the west. Late in the afternoons, it came east through Crozet on its way to Ivy, where it reversed and returned to Staunton. Your ticket included an onboard meal that's prepared by the chef from a great little local restaurant. These train trips usually sold out three months in advance, especially the fall and spring ones.

The highlight of the east run was the tunnel through Afton Mountain, just west of Crozet. The original tunnel was blasted through 4,273 feet of granite using only black powder and a twist drill, way back in the 1850s, before the advent of dynamite. The tunnel was designed and built by a French engineer, Claudius Crozet, whom our little town is named for. At the time, it was the longest tunnel in America. Then, during World War II, a new, wider tunnel was built next to it to accommodate the increased and wider military traffic, and the old tunnel was abandoned. It was recently turned into one of the "Rails to Trails" bike and walking paths, and the coarse gravel was covered with a layer of fine gravel dust, which was more "foot and bicycle friendly."

Now, the tourist train was getting close to my location. The engineer, Robby Connors, spotted me and tooted his horn, waving at me while leaning partway out the engine's window as I returned his wave. He was the regular engineer on this run, and I met him when I took many of my employees and their families on the train as a Christmas present a couple of years ago.

As the two passenger cars passed, dozens of riders stared out of their windows through the open sliding door behind me, giving them a glimpse of my brewery's production room. It was enough of a tease that we'd had some of the passengers stop by after their ride to check us out, including Robby, who'd become a semi-regular at the bar on his days off.

Once the train passed out of sight around a curve in the tracks, I finished my beer and took a quick walk through the bar before heading over to the sportsman's club. Once there, a quick glance at the bar and dining room showed the night was off to a good start. Make that a *great* start since there was no sign of Parker. I wasn't up for dealing with her again yet. In fact, I was only going to work in my office until nine, then have dinner and hit the bed early. The couple hours of sleep I got last night hadn't been nearly enough for a full recharge of my system. I planned on making up for that.

CAM ARRIVED LATE SUNDAY AFTERNOON. I introduced him to Hitch and then took him on a tour of the club, including the bomb shelter. Then we went over to the brewery for a beer. Robby was on the return leg with the train; he honked as he passed by and saw me pulling into the parking lot in the Jeep. I explained to Cam about the train. He said, "I can see why you love living here. It's a cute little town with friendly folks. But I also understand why you like Mobjack Creek; it's so totally different than this."

I replied, "It's not that different, as far as the friendly folks are concerned—with the exception of the Cliffords, of course. But, yes, the scenery is completely different, and the topography is certainly flatter. Having a boat over there now is a great addition to my life."

"I'm sure glad that you decided to buy it and that you wanted to buy into the marina, too. I'd be screwed without your help."

"I'm looking forward to tomorrow and throwing a wrench into the Cliffords' plot."

"I am, too, but you had better watch out. Whatever Tiny has up his sleeve isn't going to be good. I think he's going to try to connect your bar fight to Billy's death."

"Yeah, but you saw the video; it wasn't much of a fight. He hit me, and I fell off my stool. I grabbed his foot when he tried to kick me, and his falling was likely because he was stoned and he just lost his balance. Clearly, I was defending myself."

"Well, you had better prepare to defend yourself even more because he's got it in for you. If he intends to arrest you, and he hasn't already had that done by the authorities here, it's because he's waiting for you to come back to Mathews County, where he and his guys have the home-court advantage. Literally."

I'd already thought about this and had taken measures last night to negate some of that advantage. "I had you send me a copy of that video file for a reason. We'll soon see if I'm going to need it or not. I'm hoping not, but I'd be betting the other way."

I'D ARRANGED for my lawyer to see us early, ahead of his usual office hours. He was one of my card players and didn't mind doing the occasional favor or two, especially with all the business I threw his way. There would be a lot more coming as I took my distillery legit.

The paperwork was fairly straightforward, and fifteen minutes later, Cam was holding a certified check for seven figures. From there, we headed straight to his bank in Mathews, swapping that certified check for an identical one with Clifford's group name listed as payee. The bank manager wanted to drag his feet on issuing the Clifford check until I showed him the name attached to the number I had cued up on my phone, ready to dial. Then I advised him that he'd better not give the Cliffords a heads-up.

Cam hadn't seen what contact I'd selected on the phone and was surprised that the manager had backed down so quickly. I winked at him right before the manager handed him the check.

From the bank, we went over to Ted Clifford's office. We caught him walking out on his way to an early lunch. The look of surprise on his face was priceless as Cam handed him the check. Too late, Clifford realized he could've stalled by not accepting it. But once it was in his hand, the debt was legally paid. Cam had followed the payoff requirements right down to the last detail. And I had been videoing this whole encounter with my phone.

He protested to Cam, "I thought you weren't going to be here until tomorrow!"

I spoke up. "Why put off until tomorrow what can be done today? Now, we just need that original note marked 'Paid In Full.'"

"I'm just on my way out to lunch. We'll have to do it some other time."

I stuck the phone in his face. "So, after that note was legally paid off, you're now refusing to hand over the canceled note?"

"What? No! I'm saying that I'm going to lunch."

"Then you're in breach of your own demand note, which states that the canceled note will be relinquished upon repayment during normal business hours. And you can see that we are still within usual and customary office hours." I put on my best scary look, puffing out my chest and squinting as I got right in his face. "You don't want this to get ugly, Clifford, trust me."

I'd gotten the drift that Ted Clifford was one of those guys who got others to do the dirty work and was only brave when he had a bunch of his crew with him. Going solo wasn't in this guy's comfort zone. Reluctantly, he turned and went back into his office, with Cam and me following right on his heels. The note was in his filing cabinet; he marked it paid and signed beneath that. He handed it to Cam with a red-faced scowl, all of this still caught on camera.

I said, "Fantastic! Now let's go over to the marina for lunch, Cam."

"You two get the hell out of my office. And you,"—he pointed at me,—"are going to learn that it's not smart to go up against me."

I smiled. "Ditto, right back atcha!"

Out in the parking lot, Cam asked, "Why the hell did you tell him where we're going to be? Now Tiny will know exactly where to come and arrest you if that's what he intends to do."

"Trust me, if he wasn't going to arrest me before, he sure as hell will now. I wanted to be able to pick a place where I'd have plenty of witnesses who would swear that I didn't resist arrest and video to back that up. I guarantee that if he caught me on the road without extra eyes around, I'd at least end up with some cracked ribs, if not more. But if he does arrest me, I won't be in custody for long."

～

WHEN WE GOT to the marina, we went to the bar, where I wrote a note I handed to Brandy. She read it and then looked at me with a confused face.

I said, "It'll be okay, don't worry."

"I hope you know what you're doing." She clearly wasn't convinced.

The truth is, I wasn't either. But the sooner we got this over with, the sooner we would know if I was right. I only ordered a soda instead of lunch because I was expecting company. I didn't have long to wait. Tiny came roaring into the parking area along with another patrol car, both with their lights flashing. He and one of his deputies raced down the dock to where Cam and I were sitting at the bar.

I looked at Brandy. "As soon as we clear out of here, text exactly what's on that note to those two numbers." She nodded, still not happy about it.

Tiny rushed in and barked, "Danny Reynolds, keep your hands where I can see 'em. I'm bringing you in for questioning about the murder of Billy Clifford."

As I'd expected, I was half shoved and half dragged to one of the waiting cars after I'd been handcuffed. I tried talking to the deputy from my spot in the back seat but was told to "shut up or else." Apparently, any conversation would have to wait until we got to the Sheriff's Office, where it undoubtedly would be recorded.

8

SEND LAWYERS, GUNS, & MONEY

As soon as the sheriff's cars were out of sight, Brandy opened the note and put the two numbers it contained into her phone. Then she typed, *Send lawyers, guns, & money — DR,* and hit "Send."

In two different parts of Virginia, Alex Phipps and Tripp Sanders read their texts. Then Tripp sent his own text while Alex made a couple of phone calls. Some prepositioned reinforcements would soon be on the way.

THE DEPUTY GUIDED me into an interrogation room. I was handcuffed with my hands behind me. He sat me down in a chair and stretched my arms around its back. Not exactly a comfortable position. Then he left me alone in this room, which was freezing. I guess it was part of their plan to soften me up. Twenty minutes later, Tiny came in.

"Reynolds, right now, a team of crime scene investigators are executing a search warrant for your boat, looking for the weapon that ya used ta kill my cousin, Billy. Make life easier on yourself an' tell me where it is."

I replied, "Why on earth would you think that I killed Billy Clifford? I didn't even know the man or have anything to do with him, much less murder him! There is no weapon to find that I know of, at least none that has anything to do with me. So, you're wasting your time."

The sheriff wasn't convinced. "You are, at th' very least, an accessory ta th' murder, Reynolds. Once my team finds that weapon, you'll go down for first-degree murder. That beatdown ya gave my cousin at the bar gave him what the M.E. called a contra-coup hematomer. Meanin' his brain bounced around from the front to the back ah his skull, makin' his reactions ah bit slow. Made it easy for somebody ta sneak up behind him an' hit him over the head later. Somebody, meanin' you."

"First off, Sheriff, the only one who got a beatdown was me, from Billy. Then I grabbed his foot as he was trying to kick me while I was down. He hit the deck all on his own; all I did was protect myself. All of that was caught clearly on the security video."

"That video is the primary piece of evidence, an' it'll be enough to convict your ass."

I shook my head, "Wrong! Instead, it will exonerate me. Billy hit me, not the other way around. You're wasting both your time and mine."

The door opened, and a nervous-looking deputy stuck his head in. "Uh, Sheriff, you've got a call."

"Can't ya see I'm in the middle of a goddamn interrogation?"

"It's the Attorney General of Virginia, sir, and he said he knew you were in an interrogation but to go ahead and interrupt you."

"Huh? Well, how the hell did he know that? An' what does he want?"

"He wants to talk to you, not me, Sheriff, so I didn't ask."

Tiny glared at the deputy and then stormed out past him, leaving him to watch me. The break from the sheriff had given me time to think. I'd been very careful to dance around the fact that Billy had, of course, died by my hand. Accidentally. Technically, I hadn't yet lied to law enforcement. Yet. But I might get to a point where that became necessary. The trouble with that was once you got started, it was hard to stop. Then there was the whole thing about having to remember everything you had already said. It was where most criminals screwed up.

Two minutes later, one very pissed-off sheriff came back through the door. "You sent a copy of that entire goddamn video to the Attorney General? How do you even know him?"

"Why are you so concerned about him seeing it anyway? You said yourself that it was your primary piece of evidence, right?" It took every ounce of willpower I had not to smile right now. Undoubtedly, the sheriff never intended for anyone beyond his own "friendly" county judge to see it, and probably only after it had been heavily edited. These days, that frigging AI can change everything.

"The Commonwealth AG an' me have got different interpretations about what that video shows. So, until my team finds the additional evidence that I know we will, your buddy, the AG, won't allow me ta charge your ass."

"Oh, you can charge me, but that will give him what he needs to have a grand jury look into you and your office. They'll also dig into any judges you might appear to be cozy with. Then, he'll start reviewing past cases and citizen complaints and trace any scent of corruption back to its source. From what I've heard, your office could use a good housecleaning.

"Sheriff, you need to think about this: if a newcomer to the area like me is hearing the whispers of collusion and corruption, how long do you think it will take the AG to dig up even more? It might even go federal, with Racketeer Influenced and Corrupt Organizations Act (RICO) implications. That's going well beyond Richmond, all the way to the Justice Department and the FBI. But if you still want to charge me, go right ahead."

Up until this point, the look on his face read hatred and rage. But at the mention of a federal RICO investigation, that rage look began to wane and was starting to be replaced by fear.

Suddenly, the door opened, and a middle-aged, impeccably dressed man in a suit and carrying a briefcase barged in, accompanied by the deputy. The suit looked at me and said, "Don't say another word." He turned to the sheriff and said, "I'm Howard Falcon, Mr. Reynolds's attorney, and this interview is over. Has my client been formally charged with anything?"

At the sound of Falcon's name, Tiny's eyes widened slightly. "No. Not yet. This is just a voluntary interview."

"Then we are leaving. Wait, why is he handcuffed?"

"Standard procedure."

"Yes, if he was under arrest or being detained, not for someone who is supposedly here cooperating voluntarily. Get those things off of him."

The sheriff begrudgingly motioned for the deputy to remove the manacles. I rubbed my sore wrists after I was loose.

Falcon asked me, "Mr. Reynolds, were you read your Miranda rights?"

I shook my head. "No."

"Did the sheriff or any of his deputies inform you that you were free to leave?"

Again, I shook my head. "No, they did not. Kind of hard to leave with my hands cuffed behind the chair back."

Falcon glared at Tiny. "Do you even know how many violations of my client's Miranda rights you have committed? He has just cause to institute a huge civil case against you and your department!"

I said, "Mr. Falcon, I don't really want to hurt this county or this department by filing a lawsuit. But I don't want to be further harassed, either."

Falcon reached into his shirt pocket and produced a card, which he handed to Tiny. "In that case, we'll want a little insurance. Sheriff, send my office a complete and unedited copy of this entire interrogation," he motioned to the two cameras that were mounted on the wall just below ceiling height. "And I want copies of any body cam footage as well."

"We don't use body cams," Tiny replied.

"Then, any other videos you might have: car, parking lot, hallways, everything. If we don't receive it by close of business, I'll strongly advise my client to revisit his decision not to file suit."

Falcon and I filed out, and he turned to me and put a finger to his lips as we walked down the hall and out the front entrance. Several deputies watched as six men in black leathers and chains were waiting next to their Harleys in the parking lot. I recognized one as Tripp's right-hand guy and fellow motorcycle rider. I greeted him, "Hey, Bobby. Nice day for a ride."

Bobby grinned and said, "Tripp wanted us to make sure you got home okay."

"I will now, thanks. Counselor, where's your car?"

Falcon motioned to a large, black BMW. It was the requisite "Big Dick" defense lawyer car. We climbed in and backed out of the parking space, and then two of the loud bikes took up position in front of us while the other four fell in behind us.

Falcon said, "When Alex called me and asked me to drop every-thing and come over here, I knew it was serious. But I wasn't expecting to be part of a Hell's Angels motorcade. By the way, I'm Howard Falcon."

"I recognized you, Howard. I'm Danny Reynolds, and I'm damn glad to meet you." Falcon was widely known as the best defense lawyer in Virginia. He was also the most expensive. As happy as I was to see him show up, I wasn't looking forward to getting his bill. "Those guys work for Tripp Sanders, a good customer and security contractor, as well as a friend of mine."

"I've met Tripp. Interesting guy with a hell of a reputation."

I didn't know if he meant good or bad by that, so I just nodded. I also noticed he didn't elaborate on the circumstances behind their meeting each other, and I wasn't about to pry. Tripp could be semi-shady at times. I guess the "airplane repo business" could be like that.

Falcon continued, "Alex gave me a brief rundown of what happened. Do you mind filling in the details?"

Since it would all be privileged communication, I told him the whole story, from my getting attacked at the bar up until when he walked into the interrogation room. The only parts I left out were the ones that included Brandy's and my encounter with Billy on her houseboat.

"We definitely want all their videos. If that office is as corrupt as you suspect, we need as much insurance as we can get."

I replied, "More like the whole county. I think we shook them up a bit this afternoon, and they should leave me alone. But I agree; having you hold an 'insurance policy' is a smart move."

~

"YOU WERE SUPPOSED to grab and sit on him until after we foreclosed! You had one simple job, and you blew it! I had to pay an almost fifty-percent premium over the face value of that note in order to get it! Meaning a percentage of it is coming out of your ass, Tiny!" Ted Clifford was reacting to what Tiny had just told him. He'd gone straight over to Ted's office after releasing Danny.

"That's seven figures, Tiny, all down the drain! And I look like the biggest imbecile to those investors, meaning they won't trust me when I put together any future projects that I need them for. Goddamn it!"

Tiny hated taking crap off his cousin, and he wasn't going to put up with it anymore. "Damn it, Ted, get off my ass! Th' money isn't the worst part of it; he sicced the damn Commonwealth Attorney General on me! Then, he threatened ta get the AG to look into corruption an' possible RICO charges. Ya think they'd stop with my office? You're hanging out farther than me, pal, you an' your judges, too. Th' son of a bitch even has his own motorcycle gang protecting him. They were waitin' for him in th' parking lot. MY parking lot!

"Th' worst part is that I know he at least caused that brain bleed thing in Billy, an' I suspect he was th' one that murdered him later. But I can't prove it without doin' some more digging, an' if I do charge him, th' AG will start crawlin' up my ass."

"So, drop it, Tiny."

"But that was Billy! Our cousin!"

"Yeah, and we were both getting tired of all the trouble he was stirring up. A week ago, we were all set to foreclose on that marina and make millions on the condo project. Now you're having to sweat

72

out a possible investigation by the Attorney General, and I'm out a million bucks. Let's not make it any worse."

"Billy was a Clifford! Nobody touches a Clifford, especially not in our county!"

"Face the facts, Tiny. He was a huge liability. You were always having to cover for him. We're better off not having him around anymore. Whoever murdered him might have done us a huge favor."

"You're still talkin' 'bout a Clifford, Ted!"

"Billy was a degenerate drug addict and an embarrassment who was eventually going to end up dragging us down with him. Sometimes, you just have to cut your losses and move on."

"Maybe you do, but I don't like turnin' my back on kin."

"Then you need to start learning how! Unless you no longer like being sheriff and want to go back to catching crabs and raking oysters." Ted glared at Tiny, who glared back.

Tiny replied, "When we stop protectin' our own people, it makes me wonder why I'm still doin' this job."

"I just told you why! Billy quit being my relative when he became more trouble than he was worth. You said yourself that you hauled a ton of drugs off his boat. So, get your head out of your ass and keep a lower profile for a while. Write some more speeding tickets. I've got to come up with some kind of deal to make up for that lost million. And I don't need any distractions or complications from you in the meantime. Remember: low profile. Stay away from Reynolds for now. At some point, he'll leave us an opening so we can get the revenge you want while still having it look like our hands are clean."

9

BUG PATROL

Howard declined my offer of lunch at the marina, saying he needed to return to his office and put in some billable hours. Right, like I really believed that he wouldn't charge me for his travel time or that he wouldn't call lunch a "client meeting" in a line item on my bill.

Bobby and his fellow riders did take me up on my lunch offer, and we all descended on the outside bar. Brandy looked relieved to see me back there but also seemed curious about where the bikers fit into things.

From the far end of the bar, Hank Douglas was also staring at Bobby and his crew. Worry lines had appeared across his forehead. Hank was a regular at the bar—make that a "permanent fixture." His favorite stool was at the far end, next to the service bar. He sat there day after day with his iPad, scrolling through several dating apps.

Hank was in his mid to late sixties, about five foot six, and maybe 135 pounds, soaking wet, including his full, white beard. The women he focused on typically were half his age and usually had "daddy issues." He was pretty harmless, though the women he went out with usually ghosted him after one date. Then, he moped around for a week until he found another prospect. He was retired and lived by himself, and other than those occasional dates, this bar was the only real social life he had. I think those dating apps were more of a fantasy of his rather than him truly believing he'd find some younger woman to share the rest of his life with.

But he was also a staunch protector of Brandy, having warned me not to pull what he called a "hump and dump" on her, and threatened that if I did, I would have to answer to him. There were two reasons I wasn't too worried about that: first, it wasn't my style and not something that I'd do. Second, a sixth-grader could take Hank in a fair fight. But now I saw him staring at me with that same concerned face he wore when he issued that warning. The bar didn't often see many bikers, especially during the workweek. It was clear that they worried him. I smiled, which seemed to have no effect; his frown stayed in place. He wasn't one for change, and a bar full of bikers was definitely out of the norm.

After we finished eating, Bobby said he wanted to check on something. He went up to his bike, retrieving a few things from a saddlebag. Coming back down the dock, he motioned for me to join him. When I did, he said quietly, "Give me your phone." He took it and dropped it into one of the items he'd gotten from the bike, a small black nylon-looking pouch. I said, "What the heck?" He replied, "Just trust me. Now, we need to go check your boat for listening devices. We know they had a search warrant, but they could've had a secret one for wiretaps and bugs they wouldn't have to divulge to you, including one for your phone. Though I wouldn't put it past this bunch to do it even without a warrant."

I nodded. "Good plan. Let's go."

Over at my still-yet-to-be-named boat, Bobby began working with one of the two items he'd retrieved from his bike. It was a small rectangular black box with a digital readout on the front. He began waving it around slowly, watching the readout as he did. He turned to me, putting a finger across his lips just as Howard had done in the hallway at the Sheriff's Office. He stepped up to the helm platform, still waving the box. I watched as the numbers skyrocketed. He lifted the box higher by the VHF radio's external speaker, where the numbers began to flash.

Bobby pried the plastic cover off the speaker and removed a thin black device about the size and shape of a quarter. He took it and dropped it into that small black nylon-looking pouch. Next, he motioned toward the cabin's entry hatch. I unlocked it and let him lead the way. He found another device under the galley's tabletop and a third one attached to a lamp next to my bed. It joined the other two in the pouch with a fold-over flap that he now fastened with Velcro.

Bobby said, "That should be the last one; I'm not picking up any others. This," he indicated the pouch, "is a Faraday bag. No signals can get in or out of it. So, the bugs are still live; they just can't connect with their receiver, which should be somewhere close by. The receiver is probably connected to the marina's Wi-Fi, where it can be accessed via the Internet. These don't have enough power to transmit more than a hundred yards or so on their own."

"So, maybe from here to the bar?"

"Maybe that far, though that would be pushing it."

"Tiny is watching out for Billy's boat on the end of the dock. It's got electric power and is within the range of the Wi-Fi, probably two hundred feet away."

"That sounds far more likely."

"So much for him not harassing me anymore," I said.

"They probably thought you wouldn't think or know how to look for bugs. They will realize you do when they aren't picking up anything."

"Good. I want them to know I'm not playing around and that I have some very serious and competent professionals on my team."

"Thanks, Danny. And here, you'll need this," he said as he handed me the bug detector. "Once they realize their bugs are gone, they might try planting more. You might want to dump those first three in the water, too. Then, keep the Faraday bag for your phone. If you need to have a confidential conversation in person with anyone, put your phone and the other person's in the bag until you're through. And I can pretty much guarantee now that your phone has a wiretap on it. Voice and text will both be compromised." He reached into his pocket and pulled out a small cell phone. "Burner phone, totally clean. Business as usual on your old phone, and anything confidential, use this one."

"Thanks, Bobby."

"Ha! Don't thank me. Tripp is gonna add all this to your bill," he grinned.

I said, "It's funny; Tiny said his department doesn't have body cams, but they have money for bugs and electronic surveillance gear."

Bobby said, "That's not surprising. If they all wear body cams, it will be harder for them to get away with doing anything illegal themselves. Not turning them on is a dead giveaway that they were up to something."

"Yeah, I guess that makes sense. Another example of Clifford watching out for his own ass instead of his deputies."

The two of us returned to the bar, where I paid the bill, and then we parted ways.

After Bobby and the crew rode off, Hank addressed me. "I didn't have you pegged as somebody who's friends with a motorcycle gang. They aren't gonna start hangin' around here now, are they?"

I laughed. "You don't need to worry, Hank; they won't be moving in on any of your little friends." I pointed at his iPad. "They live pretty far from here, though they said it made for a nice one-day lunch run. So we might see them again on some weekends."

"What are they, drug dealers? Runnin' around on Monday when the rest of the world is at work."

"No, they're not drug dealers, and they were working. They're 'security consultants.'" I put air quotes around that last phrase.

"You hired them," Hank stated.

I nodded. "They've worked special jobs for me for a few years. I thought it would be a good idea to have them around this afternoon for a bit, at least until I got clear of Tiny."

"How'd you manage that?"

I replied, "Like I said, they helped. Plus, Howard Falcon explained the facts of life to him." I couldn't help but grin as Hank's eyes got wide.

"The big attorney from Richmond? The one that got the case against the former governor thrown out of court? Damn, that couldn't have been cheap."

I agreed, "It was an expensive day, for sure. But freedom is worth every cent, and too many of our troops have paid a much higher price than I just did."

Hank nodded. "Well said there, Danny."

Brandy, who had been leaning back against the beer cooler, listening, now joined in. "So, you're totally exonerated?"

"Kind of. I mean, I should be, but it's more like a Mexican stand-off. I'll take it for now, though. I'm sure that Tiny and Ted will have something else up their sleeves at some point in the future. They weren't happy about their 'losing the marina' part of the day."

Brandy looked as relieved as I felt.

Hank said, "Wait, what marina part?"

I said, "It's a done deal, Hank. The Cliffords' note is paid off, and Cam and I are now partners."

"Didn't you two come up with this idea just a few days ago?" Hank asked.

"Yep."

"How the heck did you get it done so fast?"

"When I see a deal I like, I do my due diligence quickly and get it done. I don't like waiting around for someone else to jump my claim."

"That goes for women as well as marinas. He can be quite convincing, Hank," Brandy said with a smile.

I said, "Hey! You make me sound like a con artist."

"That's not how I meant it, Danny. It's more like you don't waste time when you make up your mind about...things."

That made me feel a bit better. "Hey, speaking of not wasting time, what are you doing for dinner?"

"It's Monday, so we don't get much business, and we close at eight. I thought I'd grab something from the kitchen here."

I said, "You know, I just bought my boat, and I've only been out on it once so far. Sunset is about eight thirty, so how about I go to town and bring back a pie from Southern Pizza? We can take the boat out into Mobjack Bay, anchor, and watch the sunset over pizza and beer."

"Sounds relaxing; I'm in. I don't have to work tomorrow, so I don't mind even being out a little later."

"We're on."

TINY CALLED the deputy that was manning the county's marine unit. "Sheriff Clifford here. I need ya ta run over ta Mobjack Creek an' take a look at that Sabre boat I told ya ta look out for." Tiny had noticed no conversations had been picked up and recorded on the Sabre's listening devices.

"How about I do it first thing in the morning, Sheriff? It's gettin' dark, and my shift is over in five minutes, so I was just tyin' up the boat for the night."

"You can do it right now, or that's your last shift, ya got it? Now, get goin'!"

"Yes, sir." That's when the deputy saw that Tiny had already hung up.

Ten minutes later, the deputy was staring at an empty slip and dreading the call he was about to make.

BRANDY and I were sitting on the raised trunk cabin on the bow, having finished our pizza, and in between beers. Now, we were leaning back against the glass windshield and each against the other. When I set the anchor here in the middle of Mobjack Bay, there had been just enough breeze to keep the bow pointed west. The sunset had been spectacular, but now the only faint light that was left came from the white anchor light above the hardtop, spilling down on the deck around our feet, leaving the rest of us in the shadows.

Brandy now repositioned herself, switching to lying across my chest with her head up by my shoulder. Then she took my arms and wrapped them around her. "You know what's funny, Danny? It's so easy to take things like this for granted: something as simple as a sunset. It's been over two years since I watched one from the water. I'd almost forgotten how beautiful they can be."

I chuckled. "I had a similar conversation with a tourist at the brewpub last year. She was remarking about how beautiful our mountains were. I see them every day, so I guess I take them for granted. But she made me stop and take another look."

"She was probably trying to get you to look at her."

I asked, "What, are you jealous?"

"I didn't know you then, so no."

"Ah. But you do now..."

"Fine. Call me and let me know if she does it again."

"Like I said, she was a tourist that was just passing through."

"So, in that case, I'm not jealous." She snuggled in tighter, and I stroked her hair.

Slowly, the stars began to come out. There was no moon tonight, making them brighter and revealing more of them than ever. It helped that there were no cities or towns around the bay's edge, meaning the only light pollution came from a handful of waterfront homes a couple of miles away.

I said, "Twenty years ago, the night sky above Crozet was like this. The only light pollution was the orange glow from Charlottesville, twelve miles away. In the winter, we could see the white light halo in the sky above Wintergreen Ski Resort fifteen miles away when they were making snow. Now, thousands of new homes later, that's all just a memory. Only the brightest stars can break through the light haze. If you want to see stars, you have to go up to the Blue Ridge Parkway on top of the mountains and get away from it."

Brandy said, "That's so sad."

I nodded, then saw the first streak of light in what would turn out to be an amazing meteor shower. "Whoa!"

We were both silent, watching as the universe began an increasingly impressive celestial light show; it was truly incredible. During one of the more spectacular meteors, I could see Brandy's face as she watched in awe. She looked at me, and I saw her face change as our eyes locked and the glow faded. Our lips found each other's in the dark; then our hands began slowly working on each other's clothing. We made love on the cabin top, the only two people for miles around; the world was ours alone.

As we eventually rested in each other's arms on that hard cabin top, Brandy sighed. "I don't want to go back in."

"I can't say the same." I laughed when she swatted me in the darkness.

"I'm serious. Why don't we stay out here at anchor and go back in tomorrow? It's my day off."

"We can do that, but I want my nice, soft bunk. As great as the scenery is, this cabin top is getting hard."

"Hopefully, that isn't the only thing..."

YOU'D THINK it would be silent, waking up in a boat, but it wasn't. Small waves from the breeze that had sprung up overnight now gently lapped at the fiberglass hull. My anchor rode intermittently creaked in protest against the bow's deck cleat. Yes, that's called a rode. I originally called it a rope, but Brandy corrected me since it's attached to the anchor. I guess I had a lot to learn about boat terminology.

I listened intently, hearing the gentle clicks and snaps of underwater marine animals that were barely audible above all this other noise. Brandy's face was inches from mine; her head rested on my outstretched arm, which was almost numb. I watched as she awakened, looking at me curiously.

"What," I asked.

"It took a minute to realize where I was."

"And who you were with?"

"Nope. Knew that part," she said as she snuggled in closer. "There's not a real long list of candidates," she said as she grinned.

I felt a momentary twinge of jealousy over the idea that there might be any others on that list, but until now, neither of us had suggested any kind of exclusivity. Still, I couldn't let what I perceived as a jab go without retaliation. "Whatever you say, Parker."

The change in her eyes was instantaneous. Whether it was anger or jealousy on her part, I wasn't sure. She said, "Hey! Not funny."

Apparently, it had been a combination of anger and jealousy, so I grinned and said, "Neither was the part about my being on a list."

She raised up on one elbow, staring down at me. "What, like you don't think there are any other guys who would love to take your place right now?"

"I don't doubt it. But I don't have to like the idea, and I don't want to know who they are. I'm enjoying spending time alone with you right now."

Her eyes softened. "Good, because I am, too."

Wanting to switch topics and avoid any potential relationship landmines, I said, "I should have done this years ago."

"What! I'm your first time? Wow, you could've fooled me!" Her eyes sparkled as the corners of her mouth turned up in a sly grin.

So much for changing the subject. "Funny lady. I meant buying a boat. I've never slept aboard a boat before when it was anchored out instead of being tied up at a dock. It's a pretty unique experience that I think I'd like getting used to."

"Danny, never make the mistake of thinking of your boat as only a floating apartment. I even manage to take my houseboat out several times a year; I just have to pick my days because it isn't as seaworthy as this boat."

She continued, "Back in high school, I had a friend with a wall poster of a ship on the horizon at sunset. The caption under it read: *A ship in a harbor is safe, but that's not what ships are made for.*' Think of this one as an adventure machine. It can take you to so many places if you let it. You just need to use your imagination."

I replied, "There isn't anywhere else I'd rather be right now and no one else I'd rather be here with."

"Okay, then imagine doing more of this."

"With you."

"Well, yes, I hope so. Because I could say the same thing." She paused before asking, "So, you aren't planning to bring any of your Crozet women down here with you?"

"I hadn't planned on it. Why? Should I? Are you tired of me already?"

"No, I'm just checking."

I'm thinking that two can play this game. "In that case, are you planning on going back to your 'list' of beaus when I'm not around?"

She tilted her head slightly and said, "I thought you said you were going to be around more often."

"I will if I'm on the top of that list."

That turned out to be the wrong thing to say, as her face became clouded. "I haven't really dated anyone since the...incident with Tiny and the deputy happened. Not that I haven't been asked out; it's just that it made it hard to trust...anyone. You were the first guy I decided to take a chance on. Then, you earned my trust when you jumped in when Billy attacked me. I guess that's why I got so upset when that Parker chick pulled her little stunt. It made me question if I shouldn't have trusted you after all. That put me back in the land of insecurity. So, I was just kidding about having a list. If I did, you'd be the only one on it."

She put her head down on my chest, turning away from my face. I was glad she wasn't looking at me right then because I was having a tough time sorting out what she'd just told me. "Sorting out" might not be the best phrase; maybe I should say "absorbing" instead. I hadn't had a clue about her self-imposed two-year celibacy. To be honest, I liked the way things had been going, even if they'd gotten there pretty fast. Now I felt a little pressure that I hadn't been counting on, and I guess the mental tension had now translated into the physical type, and Brandy felt it.

"Did I say something wrong?" she asked, still facing down.

"No." Short answers usually mean they're insincere bullcrap, so I wasn't going to leave it at that. "I didn't realize..."

She interrupted, "That I was a sexual and relationship hermit?" She turned to face me, and I was relieved to see her smiling.

"Uh, yeah, I guess."

"Don't worry, Danny, this doesn't change anything or mean you have any responsibility to me. We're having fun, and if that's as far as it goes, at least you've helped me to be open to trusting people again." She kissed me, and then she rolled out of bed before going into the head.

It's funny; I freaked out a little at first when I thought she might be looking for more of a relationship. But now that she said she's open to trusting people again, that pressure I had felt changed to... well, I'll admit it...jealousy. I did feel some sort of responsibility to her, but it was more than that; it was more like we were building a connection that I didn't want to come undone. Maybe it had to do with us sharing a traumatic event that night with Billy, but I was beginning to believe it might be something more.

I climbed out and sat on the foot of the bed, waiting for her to come out of the head. When she did, she gave me a kind of self-conscious look. Whether it was the content of our conversation or the fact we were both out in the open, naked, I wasn't sure. I held out my hand and pulled her to me when she took it.

I said, "So, neither of us has a list."

She hesitated a moment, then smiled and said, "I was never good at making lists anyway."

10

GUMBO

I had Brandy run the boat on the way back in. Part of the reason was that she was more familiar with the water. But the larger part was because I wanted to share things with her. There was nothing worse than one person in a relationship making all the decisions or hogging the wheel, be it in a car or a boat. Since we'd finally figured out we were in a continuing relationship, there needed to be an equal amount of give and take.

I also wanted her to get used to how the Sabre handled. If something happened to me when we were out in the boat, I wanted her to be able to take over, including being able to dock us. I had a friend who fell and broke a leg when he and his girlfriend were doing some hiking up on the Blue Ridge. They'd driven up to their favorite spot in his vintage sports car. She managed to get him back to the car, but that was as far as she could help him. She'd never learned to use a manual transmission and couldn't drive it to the hospital. Fortunately, another couple happened by, and one of them drove the car there.

Don't get me wrong, I'm not saying that Brandy was helpless. She knew so much more about boats than I did, but each boat handles differently, and her houseboat was about as far from the Sabre as it could get. Being familiar with my boat just made good sense.

Before we got back to the creek, I asked her, "How about putting a couple of changes of clothes and a swimsuit aboard?"

With a wry grin, she replied, "You realize I only live ten feet away, right?"

"Yeah, and do you realize I'm more of a spur-of-the-moment kind of guy? I make my share of plans, but take last night, for instance. Neither of us had planned to stay anchored out. Isn't it better to be prepared for whatever might happen?"

"Oh, you mean like your rapidly dwindling supply of condoms, right?" Her grin had now gotten wider. I liked this side of her, being comfortable enough to rib me about almost anything.

"Kind of. And thanks for reminding me to pick up some more." *Two can play at this game*, I thought.

"Pretty sure of yourself, aren't ya, bucko? How many times have I told you not to expect sex every time you come over here?"

"Fewer times than we've ended up in bed. But in my defense, I'll go with that whole Boy Scout thing. Better to have one and not need it than vice versa, wouldn't you agree?"

"Don't get cocky, pal. Pun intended."

"I didn't say I was going to buy a warehouse-club-sized pack! That's not the only reason I like being with you. I look at sex between us like Jimmy Buffett looked at gumbo."

"Say *what*?" The face she made was priceless.

"You know the lyric; 'It's a little like religion and a lot like sex; you should never know when you're gonna get it next!'"

"Just for that, I'm going to keep you guessing." She shot me another sideways look.

I replied, "I love surprises."

"We'll see about that."

I was about to eat my words. A faint wailing sound was coming from behind us. I turned to look and saw the county's marine unit coming up on our stern with its blue light flashing and siren blaring.

"Uh-oh, we've got company. Better throttle back, Brandy."

She turned and looked back and then slowly began reducing our speed. She shifted into neutral as the deputy pulled alongside.

A gruff-faced deputy tied his boat to ours and said, "This is a courtesy safety examination. Do you mind if I come aboard?"

Courtesy, my ass. I asked, "Would it matter if we did?"

"Not really. You're already going to get one citation, so this gives me the right to board you."

"A citation? For what!" I exclaimed.

"No vessel registration or name documentation. You don't have to have state registration numbers on the hull if your vessel name is documented with the Coast Guard, but by law, you have to have one or the other."

I protested, "I just bought it! I haven't had a chance to change the documentation yet or add the new name."

"And you would be fine within the grace period if you have the old owner's documentation, plus the old name and hailing port still on the hull. You can make your changes on the Coast Guard website. Being a part owner of a marina, you ought to know all this."

I stayed quiet because I couldn't argue the point further. Even though he'd delivered this in a really condescending tone, he was right on the law. And I apparently now had a target on my back; otherwise, how could he have known I was part owner in the marina? I glanced at Brandy and could see the fear in her eyes. I realized she was likely reliving the incident from two years ago and was now staying silent because of it. I winked at her, hoping it would be reassuring. It didn't look like it was.

"Okay, let's do a check of all your required safety gear."

Forty-five minutes later, after taking his own sweet time, the deputy stood in the cockpit, writing my citation for no registration. I could tell he'd liked to have been able to hit me for more than that; probably so he could show off a "trophy" to Tiny, but at least he got me for something.

"Okay, Reynolds, here's your citation. You can mail the check or pay it online at this website. Until you get the documentation updated, this vessel is to stay tied up at the dock, understand? If you are out in it again before that happens, you'll get another citation with a much larger fine for a repeat offense. Do you have any questions?"

I shook my head, not trusting what I might say if I didn't stay silent like Brandy was. The deputy handed me the paper, and without so much as a "Have a nice day," he boarded his boat and untied it from us.

I went over to Brandy and put my arms around her. "Hey, you all right?"

She took in a deep breath and said, "Yeah. I just don't trust Tiny's private army."

"That's a healthy case of distrust, and I've caught it, too." I sighed as I continued, "Now I have even more to do today."

"What?"

"I'm going to need to go into Gloucester and get a vinyl boat name cut. There's no sense in having a boat I can't use."

"I thought you hadn't decided on a name yet?"

"I did this morning, and you helped."

"What? How did I do that, and what is it?"

My turn to rib her. With a huge grin, I said, "Let's just say that it was inspired by you, and it's going to be a surprise."

She frowned. "Unlike you, I *hate* surprises. So, what is it?"

"Nope. You'll just have to wait."

"In that case, I'll go with you into Gloucester while you order it. I need to go to the grocery store anyway. Besides, I've been wanting to drive Sassy again." Sassy was the nickname she'd given my Jeep.

"Just don't expect that I'll let you drive her every time I come over here," I said, jokingly paraphrasing what she told me earlier. "Crap! Now you've got me calling it a 'her.'"

"Because she's a she, and your subconscious has already accepted that." Brandy looked at me and raised her eyebrows, smiling as she said it. I couldn't help but laugh as I slowly shook my head in surrender.

"Miss McDonald, you are quite the piece of work."

"You're not exactly a boring boyfriend yourself, Mr. Reynolds."

Getting called a "boyfriend" caught me kind of off guard, though I guess it shouldn't have. My sudden smile silently confirmed this to her.

~

BACK AT THE MARINA, we had a large, late breakfast. With so much to accomplish today, now we'd have no reason to stop for lunch. The two waitresses who were working had a series of almost-whispered conversations while often glancing in our direction, obviously talking about us, something that was not lost on Brandy. Her forehead wrinkled slightly, and she finished her food in silence.

After we left the marina, Brandy drove timidly within the confines of Tiny's fiefdom, aka Mathews County. But once we crossed over into the sanctuary of Gloucester County, she had me holding onto Sassy's roll cage for dear life. She wasn't kidding about having been looking forward to driving my Jeep again, and now that she was, she didn't spare any of that added horsepower. However, I wondered if any of this might be connected to working out frustration over being talked about by our breakfast servers.

I thought a dose of humor might work well here. "I'd like to live at least long enough to put the name on my boat's stern, Brandy!"

She laughed, thankfully still staring straight ahead at the traffic she was now threading her way through. The joke had seemingly lightened the mood a bit, and she backed off the accelerator slightly. Very slightly. Then she pulled into a large strip mall on Route 17 and stopped in front of an independent establishment that promised quick service on signage and vinyl lettering.

Brandy started to get out of the Jeep, but I said, "Just where do you think you're going?"

"Uh, well..." She quickly scanned the storefronts and then pointed to a boutique that sold women's clothing. "You did say that I ought to keep some clothes on your boat, and I figured I'd get something new."

"Uh-huh. Then you wouldn't have headed for the sign shop if I hadn't called you on it?"

"Uhhh, maybe not?"

"Good answer. I'll meet you at the boutique after I'm done."

I'm pretty sure I heard her say "spoilsport" under her breath as she turned toward the boutique. Ten minutes later I walked in just as she was coming out of the dressing room wearing a pair of white shorts with a floral, teal-colored top. A saleswoman hovered behind her as she looked in a full-length mirror. Brandy spotted me in the mirror as I was walking up.

"Danny, what do you think of this combination? It's between it and those two." She indicated another pair of shorts and some long pants that were lying on a chair with two other colorful tops.

I turned to the saleswoman, "We'll take all of them."

Brandy's head swiveled around towards me, frowning. "I can only get one set, Danny."

"I want you to have all of them, so they're on me."

"I don't want you to buy them." She turned to the saleswoman. "I'll take these that I have on."

"Brandy, you only need them because I suggested that you keep some spares on my boat. My idea, my bill. And don't forget a swimsuit."

The saleswoman looked nervous, not wanting to get caught in the middle. Brandy now looked very irritated.

I said, "Make you a deal; you let me pick up the tab for the clothes, and you can pay for dinner."

Her irritation seemed to fade somewhat. After a few seconds, she said, "Mexican?"

"Done deal."

The saleswoman now looked relieved, and Brandy seemed happy. Relationship crisis averted, or so I thought. The saleswoman gathered up the garments from the chair and took them over to the counter.

I shook my head slightly, chuckling under my breath. I had wanted to buy the boat so I could have a place where I could relax and get away from my business pressures. I hadn't counted on getting into a new relationship and the pressures that now came with it.

"What?" Brandy asked.

"Uh, nothing?"

She was staring at me silently, determined to get an answer. I said, "Okay, I was thinking that life can lead you in strange directions at times."

"Oh? Now I'm strange, am I?"

"No, no, no. But think back a month ago to how your life was, how my life was, and how different each of them is today."

"Yeah, I guess." She still looked at me funny.

"I didn't mean that in a bad way. I just, well, never mind." A smart man knows to quit when he's behind. A smarter man wouldn't have said anything at all.

Now she looked amused. "I knew what you meant. Different, like better. At least from my viewpoint."

I nodded.

She said, "How about helping me pick out a bikini?"

"Yep, definitely better," I replied.

AFTER HAVING a few hundred dollars spent on a gift of clothes for them, there are a lot of women who would've at least taken a guy's arm or shown him affection in some way as they walked out of the store. But Brandy wasn't just any woman. In fact, she wouldn't even let me open the shop's door for her; instead, she barged on ahead, leaving me to fend off the door for myself.

At first, I thought she was still irritated that I'd insisted on paying. Then I realized it was just her way of being independent and showing that she wasn't in any way going to be bought or bribed. I liked this about her, so there was no way I'd be bringing up that subject again.

She drove us to a grocery store, where she took one cart for herself and shoved another at me, silently letting me know I was responsible for paying for my own food, not hers. I wasn't going to argue. Then, an hour later, we were back in the Jeep, headed back to the sign shop. I'd paid extra for expedited service, and when I walked back in the door, I saw they were just finishing up. I walked back to the Jeep with what looked like a three-foot rolled-up paper tube.

"Can I see that?" Brandy asked.

"Nope. In fact, I think I had better put it in the back."

"Don't you trust me?"

"I told you that it's a surprise. You get to see it after it's on the boat. So, don't I trust you? With almost everything. Except for this."

"Spoilsport!"

I was right; that was what she'd said earlier. I smiled until she hit the accelerator again.

BACK AT THE MARINA, I waited until Brandy took her laundry up to the laundry room next to the pool, and then I got started applying my new boat name to the transom. She returned an hour and a half later, pausing on the dock behind my boat. I was working from the swim platform and had the transom door open, partially obscuring the name.

"MBO? What the hell is that?"

I grinned as I now swung the door shut, exposing the preceding GU.

"*GUMBO*? Why on earth would you name your boat *GUMBO*?" she asked.

"I wanted to name it something that had a hidden meaning. In this case, for both of us." I could see she was lost. "From those lyrics: '...*you should never know when you're gonna get it next...*'"

"Not funny, Reynolds." She glared at me and continued to her boat, going into the cabin without another word.

Okay, I'm not the most sensitive type, and I guess I should have anticipated how this might not go over well, but the truth was, I hadn't even given it a thought; I'd just found it funny. I finished by installing the hailing port of Mobjack Creek, VA, under the name.

Brandy still hadn't emerged by the time I was done. I went over to her boat and knocked on the door.

"Come in."

I opened the door and found her standing over an ironing board in the middle of the cabin. She didn't look happy to see me.

"What did I do wrong?"

She put the iron in the stand attached to the board and focused her attention solely on me. "It's not you as much as it's us. Remember those waitresses from this morning? The ones that were in the corner, whispering? Cam just let me know their little conversation had spread to the rest of the staff about how I was screwing the new partner just to get ahead. Danny, I have to work with those people. Then you paid a lot of money for these clothes and named your boat *GUMBO* about not knowing whether or not you're always gonna get laid."

I was crestfallen. "That was supposed to be a private joke between me and you."

"Yeah, private until you slip and tell the first person about it, then it'll spread through here like wildfire, making it look like those two were right about me after all, that I'm some kind of cheap hustler that can be bought with clothes and trinkets."

I said quietly, "I really liked buying you those clothes. First, because I could; that cash came from my moonshine stash, and there is so little I can do with it without leaving a trail. And second, because you were going to leave them on my boat, meaning we are planning on doing a lot more things together. Now you've got me wondering if you're still up for that?"

"I think I need some time to figure out how I can deal with this and to decide if I can find a balance between all the work and relationship stuff. Or not."

I offered, "I'll change the name of the boat to something else if that helps. And for the record, I was never going to tell anyone about the meaning behind it; that was strictly private. Plus, I'm a big fan of gumbo, so it fits. And we had already planned on going out before I ever entertained any thought of buying into the marina. Ted Clifford didn't call Cam's note until after that."

Brandy replied, "A fact which they don't know and probably wouldn't believe anyway. I knew that this might eventually happen; I just didn't know how fast it would or how bad it would turn out to be. I'm supposed to manage all the bartenders and the servers. Kind of hard to manage people who don't respect you. So, I think I'm going to need to take a break."

Brandy took the iron out of its stand and went back to smoothing out wrinkles while looking away from me. I wished I knew how to smooth out our relationship wrinkles.

I turned and left without a word. Once I was back on the dock, I looked at my watch. Three o'clock. Somewhere out over the Atlantic, it was five. This time, the Buffett reference didn't seem funny. I glanced at the lettering on my stern as I passed and decided to come up with something else. Removing the letters so soon after they'd been applied would be easy enough, but first, I needed to apply something else to me. Alcohol.

11

GETTING CUT OFF

I t was slow this early on a usually slow day of the week. Hank was the only customer. Not wanting company or conversation, I sat at the far end of the bar, on the opposite end from where he was. I didn't know this bartender yet, but from the look I got, it was clear that she knew me. To her, I was the predator owner, and the new path to getting promoted around here apparently ran right through my bed from what she'd heard. I ordered a beer with a side shot of whiskey.

"I thought you'd be doin' something with Brandy, this being her day off and all," Hank said from the far end of the bar.

"Hank, please just drink your beer and leave me alone."

"Uh-oh, trouble in paradise already?"

"Hank, shut the hell up, and drink your damn beer." I no longer felt the need to be diplomatic about it.

The bartender put my drinks in front of me while eyeing me warily. I concentrated on the liquids, barely looking at her. After taking a gulp of beer, I chased it with the whiskey shot, then motioned for her to refill the small glass.

I know what you're thinking; *liquor won't help anything.* Well, in this case, it wouldn't hurt anything, either. Besides, I had little to lose at this point. By the time my shot glass had been refilled, the first one had already given me a warm glow that reached from the top of my head down to my stomach. Now I gave that warm feeling a booster shot.

Forty minutes later, Brandy showed up. By then I had my sixth shot and my third beer sitting in front of me.

"I didn't think you were the type to go on a binge whenever you hit a bump in the road," she said, standing next to me.

I held up my right hand's pointer finger. "I don't think of myself as a 'type.' Bump in the road, you say. Sounded a lot more like 'Bridge Out' to me. An' I'm makin' some new friends. This is Sam Adams, an' this is Jack Daniels. Say hello, boys. Oops, Jack, it's time for you ta go." I downed the shot while Brandy scowled at me.

"Brandy, I told him that he ought to be out doing something with you, or even better, staying inside doing something with you," Hank said, grinning.

"Shut up and drink your goddamn beer, Hank!" This time it didn't come from me; it was Brandy.

The bartender moved down closer to Hank, and away from her manager. At the same time, Cam came out of the restaurant and made a beeline for Brandy, having seen her on the security cam.

"Hey, Brandy, I know it's your day off, but would you mind taking the bar for a few minutes while I borrow Sue? Oh, hey, Danny."

I raised my empty shot glass silently in acknowledgment.

"Uh, sure, Cam." Brandy went around and swapped places with the woman I had now learned was named Sue, who disappeared into the restaurant with Cam.

Brandy came over and stood in front of me, frowning. "How many is that for you?" She motioned to the shot glass.

"Not nearly enough if I can still count. Which means I need 'nother." I was beginning to slur my words, and my movements were no longer as smooth and coordinated as they should be.

"Not while I'm behind the bar. You're cut off."

"I know. That's the reason I started drinking in the first case."

Down at the far end of the bar, Hank was taking a sip of his beer, which now spewed over the bar as he laughed. Brandy glared and threw a bar towel at him. "Clean that up!"

"Sheesh! I gotta find a new bar, one where I don't get yelled at all the time," he said.

"Right, like any other bar would have you," Brandy said. She moved down the bar, stopping halfway between me and Hank, leaning back against the beer cooler, ignoring me.

I turned the empty shot glass upside down, putting it on a coaster. It had already done its job. Five minutes later, Sue returned with the two waitresses from earlier. The trio looked sheepishly at Brandy and stole glances at me as well.

One of them said, "Brandy, Cam set us straight. We're sorry about what we said earlier, we didn't know you two were already dating before Mr. Reynolds decided to buy into the marina."

Brandy shook her head. "It's not just what you said, but what you were willing to believe about me. I thought all of you knew me better than that. But what's done is done; we'll just have to see how things go moving forward." She glanced at me as she got out from behind the bar.

I can't blame Brandy a bit for not totally letting them off the hook. If they were going to get back to a higher level of trust, they'd have to work for it. But now they moved down to where I was. The same one who had done the talking addressed me.

"Mr. Reynolds, Cam told us what you did for him and us. Thanks for saving this place and our jobs."

"Ahm, my name's Danny. But glad ta do it. Sue, how's about givin' me my tab so I can get outta here."

Sue looked confused. "There's no tab—you own the place."

"Nah, I only own half the place, an' I don't steal booze from my partner."

The original pair went back inside while Sue brought the bill which I paid in cash, leaving a very generous tip. I hope she felt guilty about the tip because of what she also apparently had believed of Brandy and me. Or, maybe she thought I left it to try to impress her and get into her pants, too. At this point, I wouldn't have cared less what she or anyone else thought, even if I had been sober.

Brandy came up to me. "Give me your keys."

"Wait, you don't want me anymore, but you still want my Jeep?"

"I never said I don't want you; I said I needed some time to decide how to work things out. And I want your keys to keep you from hurting yourself or anybody else."

"Nah, ya said IF you could work things out, not how. Two toootally different things. You said you wanted a break, so, take all th' time ya want, cause mebbe I need one too. An' take th' Jeep, I don' need ta worry about ya hurtin' anybody with it; you already done far worse without it. In fact, keep th' sonofabitch; it's yours." I tossed my keys on the bar and began stumbling my way back to my boat.

I woke up in my bunk with no idea what time it was other than nighttime since the cabin was completely dark. I went to look at my watch, then realized it was gone. My shoes and clothes were gone, too. For a split second, I thought I'd been rolled by a mugger, but I realized I was tucked in under the covers. My head was fuzzy as hell, but I knew enough to realize somebody had to have put me here.

From somewhere in the darkness next to me, a voice said, "It's well past midnight; go back to sleep." Then, an arm reached over and half-hugged me. Brandy, of course. Then I did what she suggested as my consciousness faded away.

Sunlight was streaming into the cabin as I awakened with an arm still draped across my chest. Slowly the events of yesterday refocused themselves in my brain, not being helped by the guy using the jackhammer inside my skull. My eyes followed the arm back to the torso and then the head that was also attached to it. Brandy was lying next to me, looking at my face.

"Hey. How do you feel?" she softly asked.

Instead of answering what was an obviously stupid question, I asked her, "What are you doing here?"

The arm pulled back. "I followed you to make sure you got aboard okay. It was a good thing, too, because you fell down the companionway steps and were out cold. I managed to get you up into bed, then stayed here to make sure you were all right. Just like you did for me that night Billy tried to..."

I interrupted her, "Right, thanks for that. So, we're even now. And as you can see, I'm fine, just hungover."

She was taken aback. "So I guess that means I'm dismissed?"

"If you mean like you dismissed me yesterday, I'd say so, yeah."

"I didn't dismiss you, Danny! I said I needed time to figure out how to deal with both work and us."

"You said IF and that you needed a break from me, or us, what-ever! I've learned that whenever a woman tells me that she needs to take a break to figure things out, that's code for 'I'm permanently breaking up with you, loser!' We were barely together anyway, so I don't know why I should feel so upset. It's not like I really meant anything to you, or you wouldn't have tossed me away like trash."

"I tossed you away like trash? You plastered your boat's transom with a word that implied I was your round-heeled bed buddy at your beck and call, and that's all I'm good to you for! And you tried buying me off with clothes like I'm some kind of cheap whore!"

I said softly, "I told you I wanted to pick a name that would mean something to both of us, like our own private joke. And I wasn't trying to buy you; I wanted to do something nice for you, with no strings attached."

Her face was getting redder with anger as she said, "No strings attached, my ass! In fact, they were attached to my ass! You might recall your little caveat; the one that says those outfits were to be kept aboard this boat. So then you could dress me up like your own personal little show pony if we went somewhere. I'm your private joke, Danny, just fun and games on a string, like a marionette."

"No, Brandy, you were someone I had already begun to fall for, but now I can see that was only one-sided. You never really knew me at all, or you'd have never for a second believed that crap. That's simply not me. But I'm sorry you feel that way and truly sorry the boat name offended you. I'll get it off there today, so you don't have to look at it anymore as you walk by."

I swear her blue eyes got a shade darker as she looked into mine. Was that a sign of regret? Sadness? Anger? Maybe a little of all three. I hoped so—not to be mean, but because I felt a boatload of those emotions myself. Misery loves company, so they say.

Without a word, she got out of bed. She'd only been wearing panties, and now she put on yesterday's clothes for her ten-foot walk of shame between our boats, though there was no shame involved this time.

As she left, she turned and said, "I put Sassy's keys on the galley counter." I saw a single tear tracing a path down her face before she quickly turned back away and walked out.

MY SHOWER HADN'T HELPED my condition as much as I'd hoped. I still had a pounding head and an aching heart. I looked at the galley but didn't even bother to open the fridge despite all the fresh groceries waiting inside. Part of the reason I was originally attracted to this place was the restaurant, so I decided to let somebody else cook today. This is why I was now sitting at a table by a window, sipping fresh orange juice and awaiting a plate of sausage gravy and biscuits.

My number one hangover cure is a McDonald's quarter-pounder with cheese, fries, and a Coke, but the nearest McDonald's was many miles away, and I felt like I would die before I could drive there. Besides, sausage gravy and biscuits were a close second. The freshly squeezed juice closed the gap between the rankings of those cures.

I was facing over toward the door, and that was why I saw Brandy come in. She glanced around the dining room before spotting me and quickly looking away, then she disappeared through the swinging kitchen doors. She reappeared two minutes later, carrying two plates of sausage gravy and biscuits. I was surprised when she headed to my table.

Brandy set one plate down in front of me and asked, "Can two hopefully still friends have breakfast together?"

I replied, "Some say a friend is someone who knows your true nature but likes you anyway. Yesterday showed that we hadn't really learned the true nature part."

"You mean we haven't yet, not hadn't, Danny."

"I'm pretty sure I had the right tense...as in past tense."

"If that's how you want to leave it."

"If I recall correctly, I wasn't the one making those decisions."

"Danny, this plate isn't getting any lighter, and I would really like to eat my breakfast before the gravy congeals." Her face was hopeful.

I waved to the chair opposite mine but didn't stand like I normally would've.

"Thank you," she said as she sat down.

I nodded, looking down while starting to make my high-carb hangover cure disappear. The effects hadn't quite kicked in yet. I started to reach for my juice but saw that Brandy was now taking a sip of it.

She looked over at me and asked, "You don't mind, do you?"

I shook my head, holding back the smart-assed remark I was thinking. I wondered if this was some kind of test or something like it. Maybe proving a point? It wasn't like I really had an effing clue. Yesterday sure proved that. The problem was that I shouldn't care at this point. I didn't want to, but I still did. Damn it.

She set my juice down and looked at me. Softly, she asked, "Did you mean it when you said you were falling for me?"

"What difference does that make now."

"It would make a lot of difference to me."

No way I was answering that and getting it thrown back in my face. "I thought you wanted to eat before your breakfast solidified."

I guess my non-answer did a better job of replying than I could've if I'd admitted it aloud. Suddenly, I wasn't hungry anymore.

"I gotta go." I stood up and put some bills on the table. "See you around." It was Brandy's turn not to say anything. I headed for the door.

~

THE SIGN PEOPLE were surprised to see me again so soon, but I wasn't in the mood to offer any explanation. This time, I waited in a customer chair while my vinyl was cut and outlined. I was anxious to get back to the boat and change out the name. Fortunately, I hadn't registered the "Gumbo" name yet with the Coast Guard, but I'd get that done with this one before I went back to Crozet. I decided to go back early, leaving tomorrow morning. I needed the distraction of business to get my mind off...things.

Once back at the marina, I bypassed the bar, sticking to the main dock. Brandy gave me a timid wave as I walked by, and I barely nodded in return. I went through the restaurant into Cam's office for a quick chat to let him know I was leaving a few days early.

I WAS SITTING on my swim platform, preparing to apply the new name to the transom. As I suspected, by using the heat gun that I picked up at the hardware store, the day-old lettering had peeled right off. The transom looked strange with only "Mobjack Creek, VA" in the smaller letters under where the larger letters of the name were about to go.

I unrolled the new name, removing the backing that covered the adhesive. I sprayed it and the transom with a water-based wetting agent, which allowed me to adjust the name before I used a squeegee to affix it permanently. Another type of opaque adhesive backing material was attached to the front of the letters to maintain their spacing and straightness until that point.

I lined it up according to the masking tape tabs that I measured for and placed just above where the name would go in order to keep it nice and level. Using the squeegee, I forced the wetting solution out from behind the letters, allowing me to peel off the opaque backing, leaving only the letters behind. After a couple of days, the adhesive would become almost permanent.

I climbed up on the dock to admire my work. The transom now

bore the name "*COHIBA*," my favorite cigar brand. The real ones—from Cuba. Now, to go use my laptop and register it on the USCG website, and I'd be back to being legal again. At least legal as it related to my boat. No more probable cause for searches by "Tiny's navy."

By the time I finished, it was after six o'clock. Ordinarily, I'd have a beer or a cocktail in my hand by now, but today, I thought it wise to skip those libations. A couple of minutes later, a knock on my hull interrupted my thoughts. I opened the aft cabin hatch and spotted Brandy on the finger pier, holding a beer flat loaded with takeout containers.

"Hey, Danny. Have you had dinner yet?" Her voice was almost worried and hesitant.

"I thought you were working?"

"Only half a shift. Sue needed more hours so she could cover her personal property tax bill. It's so stupid that they charge us over and over every year for our cars and boats, even after we've already paid the sales tax up front..."

"Brandy?"

"Yeah?"

"You're babbling."

"Oh, right. Well, have you had dinner yet? I got to thinking, we never did have that Mexican dinner I promised you..."

I held up my hand. "No, I haven't had dinner yet."

"Well, this is from Jose & Pepe's Cafe in Mathews, and it's fantastic. I wanted to see if you would like to share it with me."

"Settling our account?"

"Uh...no. Just wanted to see if we could have dinner and...talk."

"About?"

"About whether or not you were going to leave me standing out here on the dock while the food got cold. About us, damn it! What else did you think I would want to talk about? So, can I come aboard or not?"

I waved her aboard, then took the flat from her and put it on the table in the galley while she dug out two beers from the fridge. I know. I said I didn't want to have a beer tonight but didn't want to talk "about us" without having one first.

She set the various containers out, giving me a running commentary as she did so.

"Their salsa is great, and the chips are house-made. The guacamole is the best you'll find anywhere, and I'd put their burritos up against anyone else's. And the ceviche is to die for…"

"You're babbling again."

"No, I'm not, I'm describing."

"Okay, Guy Fieri, I get it. You babble, er, describe things when you're nervous."

"Who says I'm nervous?"

"Me. And you've never been nervous before with me; why start now?"

"Because you've never been angry with me before, Danny."

I grabbed a roll of paper towels and put it on the table, then motioned to her to sit across from me. Instead, she slid in close to me.

I said, "For the record, I'm not mad at you, I'm hurt. Two entirely different things. If I was mad, we wouldn't be sitting here together. Though, honestly, I'm not really comfortable about it."

She took a deep breath, then let it out. "Being hurt is worse."

"Tell me about it."

"I didn't mean to hurt you, Danny."

"I hope not, but it's inevitable when two people don't feel the same way about each other. Which became obvious when I should've kept quiet but didn't. I had to run my stupid mouth this morning, and it made us both feel awkward."

"I wouldn't say that."

"Oh, trust me, I feel plenty awkward right now."

"No. I mean, I wouldn't say we don't feel the same way. I just never said it out loud like you did. I'm sorry that I took the whole gumbo thing the wrong way. I'm glad you still decided to replace it with something that still has a private meaning for both of us."

That threw me for a loop. "How do you figure that?"

"You don't remember that after our first date, we sat out in your helm chair and smoked one of your Cohibas together?"

"Oh, yeah. You came over after you turned me down for a second date."

"No, after you gave up too easily and took 'no' for an answer."

"I was taught that when a lady says 'no,' it means no, regardless of what it's about. I was also taught to always hold doors for ladies and to walk on the outside of any sidewalks so that I get hit by a car instead of you. I know; I'm a freakin' dinosaur, and some would even say I'm a sexist."

"I wouldn't."

"I'm glad you don't think so because this is just me being me. I don't plan on changing anytime soon."

"Please don't, at least not on my account."

Not knowing what more to say, I grabbed a chip and went in for the salsa. She hadn't been babbling; she'd been reciting food gospel. It was every bit as great as she'd said. The guacamole was the best I'd ever tasted.

"Thanks for bringing dinner."

"Well, Cam told me you decided to leave tomorrow, and I knew I might never get another chance to tell you how I feel. I didn't want to leave things how they'd ended up."

"Geeze, are there no secrets around this place?"

"Just the ones between you and me. Otherwise, nope. The place is a gossip mill, which is how our whole misunderstanding started."

"I never pegged Cam as a gossip."

She said, "He's not. He's worried that two of his friends aren't getting along. And if it hadn't been for Cam setting the staff straight..."

I finished her sentence. "We wouldn't be having dinner together right now."

"Probably not. But I'm glad we are." She paused a few seconds, then said, "So, do we keep on seeing wherever this is headed?"

"I'm going to tell you where I'm headed, and that's right to the bottom of each of these containers. This stuff is addicting."

"I meant us."

"I know what you meant; I'm not a complete idiot. Except for how some people discern hidden meanings behind boat names."

"Some people?"

I sighed. "You."

"Well, I like this one and the memory that comes with it. That was a fun night."

"Yeah, it was."

"So, you haven't answered my question yet. Do you still want to keep seeing each other?"

"What do you have in mind?"

"Maybe dinner out the next time you're here? Then maybe another cigar afterward?"

"When are you off again?"

"Day after tomorrow, but aren't you going back to Crozet in the morning?"

"I can stay another day and go back on Saturday morning."

"Just don't plan on leaving early." She smiled. "And I really don't want to go home tonight if you don't mind me staying."

I said, "Well, I'd hate to see you have to go all the way home in the dark." Even if her home was only ten feet away.

"WE SHOULD BE in Crozet on Saturday by 9:00 a.m., local time, Uri. I've arranged for a siding in the middle of town, about ten minutes from that club."

Uri, the man's boss, nodded. He had a little more time left in Boston before they traveled to Crozet. It was a long trip by train, but he was anxious to make the acquisition and wanted to have all the amenities his private train afforded him at his disposal while he was there.

Not only was the club's property unlike anything else anywhere, but the games were big and growing bigger by the month. It would be well worth the trip, and besides, it wasn't like he was taking Amtrak to get there. His private train's interior finishes and appointments rivaled anything to have ever come out of a private jet factory or mega yacht boatyard. He was traveling in extreme luxury, albeit at ground level.

Uri smiled at the thought of adding that property to his portfolio. The features were so unique and clandestinely historic. But he was really after the games and, even more importantly, the players. Once he owned the club, he could introduce some of the most powerful players to some of the most lovely and talented underage courtesans in his employ. Each would be carefully chosen and matched with a target due to their individual talents and abilities.

He'd learned from Epstein about the persuasive value of videos of politicians and high-profile businessmen doing unspeakable things to underage girls. Leverage like this was the highest form of power, and he planned on collecting as much of it as possible, offering its use to his closest allies for a price, of course. A very steep price.

12

HANGING OUT MOBJACK STYLE

B randy and I spent parts of the next day together, both before and after her shifts. While she was busy working, I took *Cohiba* out solo, learning more about how she handled. After a bit of practice, I got pretty good at docking her singlehanded and at navigating with my large-screen GPS.

Soon after I turned into the creek channel on my way out, that same deputy in the sheriff's boat started following closely behind me. I saw him speak into his radio microphone, no doubt checking on me. *Yeah, jackass, the name is registered, and I'm completely legal now.* Soon, he dropped back, finally turning away and leaving me alone.

Things were really falling into place for me. Staying at the marina turned out to be even better than I'd hoped it would. I was more relaxed than ever, though part of that probably could be attributed to Brandy. I know what you're thinking, and no, it wasn't just sex that was relaxing me. It was because we were becoming more and more comfortable with each other following our misunderstanding, and I loved spending time with her. It was pretty clear now that she felt the same way.

Other than those two incidents with the marine unit, that was my only interaction with any of Tiny's private army of late. Now that the Commonwealth's Attorney General had put Tiny on notice, I guess he decided to let sleeping dogs lie; at least for the time being. Though I had no doubt that Ted was trying to find the best way to get some kind of revenge. He hadn't seemed the type to give up so easily, and I was pretty sure I had cost him a pile of money. I hoped I had.

I had dinner at the bar last night, hung out until Brandy closed, and then walked her home. After she complained about a sore muscle in her shoulder that she'd pulled when changing a beer keg, I began massaging it.

She groaned, "Oh, Danny, that feels so good. Don't stop doing that for at least another year or two."

"It's one of the things I'm good at. Go grab a hot shower, then lie on the bed, and I'll give you a full massage."

"You don't have to tell me twice!" She raced into the head. Five minutes later, she was stretched out on her stomach on the bed.

"You know, I could really get used to this. And even if I fall asleep, please stay here with me." She let out a low moan as I concentrated on the area that had the pulled muscle. Four minutes later, she began making a sound similar to a cat purring, but it was just her breathing through her mouth. She was completely and fast asleep.

JUST BEFORE DAWN the next morning, I heard her take an extra-large breath as she began to wake up. I said softly, "Hey, it's your day off, go back to sleep."

She turned on her side and backed up toward me, pulling my arm over her and interlacing our fingers. I pulled her even closer, with my face buried in the back of her head. We were both asleep again within a minute or so.

Two hours later, sunshine was backlighting the thin curtains of her room.

"Good morning," I said to the back of her head. We hadn't moved at all in the last two hours.

In a sad voice, she replied, "I fell asleep on you last night, Danny; I'm sorry."

"Don't be; you needed your sleep. How's the shoulder this morning?"

"Doesn't hurt anymore. That was an amazing massage."

"Like I said, it's one of the things I'm good at. I'm glad I could make it better."

She rolled over on her other side, then scooted in close to me, saying, "Let me show you a different kind of massage." She hooked one leg over me and drew me in closer as we kissed...

A WHILE LATER, I rolled onto my back, completely spent and breathless. "You're incredible."

She took a deep breath. "No, we're incredible together. I love being with you no matter what we're doing, but making love with you is right up there at the top of my list."

"Mine too."

"I'm going to miss you when you go back to Crozet tomorrow."

"It's only for a few days, then I'll be back. Besides, you know what they say: absence makes the heart grow fonder."

She rolled on her side, propping herself up on an elbow, looking serious. "I think I'm already past the point of just 'fondness,' Danny."

"I'd say we both are." I pulled her to me and kissed her.

I TOLD her we should only have a light breakfast, so over yogurt and coffee in her galley, she asked what I had up my sleeve.

I said, "The other day, you told me to think of *Cohiba* as an 'adventure machine.' So, today, we will use her for just that and go across the bay for lunch at this place I saw online. Looks like they have some really extreme bar food. Then tonight, we're going to go to the White Horse Bistro for dinner; we have reservations for eight o'clock. Today will be all about good food, great company, and an adventure out on the water."

"I love...the White Horse Bistro!" She paused again before continuing, "I bet you thought I was going to say I love *you* instead of the White Horse, didn't you?" She gave me an impish grin.

"You already did once today. No, actually twice..." I laughed as she swatted my arm.

She said, "Well, there are different ways to tell somebody you love them, you know."

"Believe me, I do. And that last one almost killed me. Ow!" I got swatted even harder.

"Okay, smartass, I know where we're going to dinner, but where are we going for lunch? That's a long way across the bay just for bar food."

"I know, but I've never done that before—crossing the bay, I mean. It's a whole new adventure! The destination is a surprise, but from what I read, the food is well worth the trip."

"I already told you that I hate surprises. But at least I finally get to do something with you that you've never done before. Ow!" She was the one who got swatted this time.

I CHECKED the GPS plotter as we exited Mobjack Bay, setting a course for the tip of the Eastern Shore. At cruising speed, we'd be there in an hour and a half. It was good that we'd slept in, or we'd be early enough for brunch instead of lunch.

As we cleared Mobjack Bay, Brandy took off her shirt and shorts, revealing her new bikini. Glancing around and seeing no boat traffic, she asked me to slow down a bit, undid her top, and grabbed some tanning accelerator.

"Rub some of this on my back and my legs, would you, Danny?"

"Wow. I knew I should've bought a boat a long time ago. Why the sudden interest in tanning? And I'll happily do your front while I'm at it!"

"Um, thanks for the offer, but I want to get where we're going in time for lunch today, not breakfast tomorrow. And the interest in tanning is your fault. Remember the last time we went to the White Horse when we ran into Babs?"

"Ah, yes, quite a memorable experience. She gave me an elbow massage at the bar with one of her; what did you call them? Boca beauties?"

"Everything about that chick is surgically enhanced in some way, except for her tan. If I recall correctly, you seemed to appreciate it, saying there were no boundaries to it. It's something she goes about as far as she can to show off without getting arrested for public inde-cency. Anyway, one of my new tops is a bit low-cut, so I thought I'd erase some of my own boundaries for you."

"I thought you already did. Ow! Never hit the captain when he's running the boat!"

"Don't make dirty jokes about those other boundaries, and I won't!"

"Back to Babs, you said that she hangs out there a lot. Are you sure this is about me, not you and her?" I grinned.

"Well, if you'd rather I dress like a nun tonight instead..."

"I'll pass; I was never really into role-playing. I love you just the way you are."

"That's good because I...what did you just say?"

"What?"

"You just said you loved me?"

"I think my main point was that I'm a fan of how you're dressed right now..."

"Reynolds, you just admitted that you love me!"

"Actually, you know that the English language can be so complex, and some words are easily misconstrued..."

I was stopped mid-sentence when she wrapped her arms around my neck and kissed me. Then she smiled and said, "You're right, so I'll make it simple enough for you to understand. Me too."

IT TOOK two and a half hours at our reduced speed until I saw the Fisherman Inlet Bridge looming not too far ahead. I turned and looked down at Brandy lying on a towel on her back on the deck. "Hey there, time to put the ol' boob holster back on, we're almost to where we are going."

She stood up and began putting on the swimsuit top. "Boob holster? Really? Only those who wear them have earned the right to call them that."

"Ta-ta binder, then."

"I'd hate to hear what you call bikini bottoms."

"View ruiners. Fabric chastity belts."

"You're incorrigible!"

"It's my mission in life to make the English language simpler and easier to understand. I think every English-speaking male past puberty would have no problem understanding the meaning of the term 'boob holster.'"

"I'm beginning to wonder if you're even past puberty."

"Thought I already proved that a couple of times this morning."

She shook her head in exasperation, then looked over my shoulder at our position on the GPS. "What's down here?"

"A place called Mallard Cove. I read that they have a couple of highly-rated beach bars that serve some wicked lunches."

"Oh yeah, I've heard of that place. I've always wanted to go there."

"You mean I've found something that you haven't yet done in a boat?"

She rolled her eyes while shaking her head. I took advantage of her distraction to pull the front of her bikini bottom down slightly. She slapped my hand.

"Hey! No, no, bad boy!"

I grinned. "Just checking. Your tanning stuff seems to be working nicely." She was noticeably several shades darker in just a little over two hours. "I'm a fan of a good tan line."

"I thought you didn't like them."

"Maybe not on some other guy's girlfriend. But yours will make finding...you...in the dark so much easier, not to mention fun!"

Now, we passed under the tall bridge, the final segment of the

Chesapeake Bay Bridge-Tunnel before it reached the peninsula, which was the Eastern Shore. Ahead on the left at the start of a medium-length beach was a large thatched-roof stage. Up higher on the beach were two corrugated sheet-metal-roofed, open-air buildings placed side by side: the Mallard Cove and Catamaran beach bars. Both looked like they were already getting filled with boaters and auto travelers who were already getting an early start on this warm summer weekend.

Brandy commented, "Wow, those look really nice."

Before I could verbalize the juvenile thought that instantly popped into my head, Brandy held up a pointer finger in front of my face.

"Don't...go there!"

I put on my best "Who, me?" look.

I slowed to idle speed as we approached the rock-lined inlet leading to the marina basin. Brandy quickly put on her shorts and shirt, then readied a couple of dock lines. I studied the inlet and judged the effect that the outgoing cross-current would have on *Cohiba* as we entered. I gave it a tiny bit of starboard throttle to help ease us through the turn, dropping back to idle again once we were safely out of the current and between the rock jetties.

"I'm impressed, Reynolds. You do this like you've done it before. And before you say it, don't!"

I smiled for a second, then quickly went back to studying the marina layout. It was a little tight in here for my liking as an amateur. We turned left again, heading for a small floating dock in the corner reserved for restaurant and bar patrons.

After I finished that turn and looked ahead, I gripped the wheel tightly. To my left was a line of bows sticking out of slips, and to my right were numerous floating docks with larger yachts tied broadside to the tee ends of each dock. While there was several times our width in open water ahead, I knew that bumping up against any of these floating works of art could mar paint jobs that could cost tens of thousands to repair.

Brandy gave me a little coaching. "You're good. Take us out of gear about a hundred feet before the floating dock, and just bump her in and out of gear as you need to without adding any throttle. There's no wind nor current, so it'll be a straight-in. The biggest, most common mistake newbie boat owners make is coming into the dock too fast. We're in no hurry. I'll put the loop end through our spring cleat, then take the bitter end with me and attach it to the dock."

"Uh-huh." There were a lot of people on the restaurant's deck, overlooking that dock and the row of charter boats next to it. There was nothing like having a big audience to make me nervous as hell.

"You've got this, Reynolds. Just go slow."

I eased up alongside the floating dock like I'd done it hundreds of times. Brandy hopped off the boat and did some line handling unlike any I'd seen before. Standing straight without bending over or getting down close to it, she whipped the line around the dock cleat. With a couple of flicks of her wrist, she made it crisscross over and over on the cleat. Then, with an added flair, she made it form a loop in midair, where it fell perfectly across the cleat. Pulling the bitter end locked it down tight. She repeated the process with the stern line. She winked at me; and then I shut both engines down.

Two older men were going past on the walkway above the landing. They stopped for a moment to admire Brandy's line-handling skills. At least, I think this was what they were admiring.

"How did you learn to do that?" I was impressed.

"A life spent around the docks. You can't help but learn a few things here and there."

"Huh, I'm impressed. I think those old guys were too. Though they might've been admiring your..." Brandy held up her pointer finger, stopping me mid-sentence, as I grinned.

I continued, "Well, let's go find out if the reviews on this place are true or not."

If the crowd was any indication, it must be good. We walked down a covered walkway between the two buildings. Ahead, there was a line ten deep at the entrance to the Catamaran and no line at the Cove Beach Bar, which was where we headed. Unfortunately, there were no open tables, either.

Next to the beach, a server appeared to be arguing with those two older guys who had watched Brandy tie us up. They were seated at a table with six chairs. The taller of the two spotted us looking for a table and waved us over. I looked at Brandy, who shrugged. We went over to the table where that man was telling the server, "See Angel? I told you we were waiting for our friends." He turned to us and said, "What took you guys so long?"

Brandy never missed a beat. "Sorry, guys. We had to finish tying up the boat."

We sat at the two chairs on the opposite side of our new "pals." The server asked us, "You two know these rascals?" It seemed light-hearted rather than mean-spirited.

I replied, "Known 'em for years. They're like family to us."

She looked doubtful but asked us what we wanted to drink. We each ordered a draft beer. After she walked off toward the service bar, the tall guy said, "Hey, thanks for saving our tails. Angel was about to evict us from this table, and we only took it because it was the last open one left. But on busy days, they like having at least half the seats filled at every table."

"Can't blame them for that," I said. "I'm Danny Reynolds, and my better half here is Brandy McDonald."

"Nice to meet y'all. I'm Sandy Morgan, and my so-called friend here is Bill Cooper, but everyone calls him Gilligan."

The shorter man exploded. "They do not, ya hack! Don't pay any attention ta him, 'cause nobody else does, either." This was delivered in a gravelly voice with a New Jersey accent.

Brandy stared at Cooper, then said, "I know you! You're that captain on the *Tuna Hunters* show; they call you Baloney!"

Morgan rolled his eyes. "Oh, great. Now we'll have to put up with his overinflated ego for at least a week."

"Yeah? Well, you're just sore 'cause nobody recognizes ya outside ah bookstores."

I said, "I knew your face was familiar! You're that author."

He looked back at Cooper, "So there; bite me, Gilligan!"

It turned out that the two had been friends for a few years. They lived on boats in a private marina next door, owned by one of the Mallard Cove partners. Cooper told the story about how the owners had purchased this place all rundown and overgrown, with crumbling docks and no beach bars, restaurants, or hotel. They had begun steadily improving the property from the first day they'd owned it.

Angel delivered our beers and then took everyone's food orders.

Brandy then told the story about our marina and how I jumped in to help save it from development.

"Kind of the opposite of what they've done here," Sandy commented.

"Totally different concepts," I agreed. "Nothing personal, but I wouldn't want to live in the middle of all this and all these people."

Sandy Morgan nodded. "It's why we live next door. It's fenced off from here but still convenient for when we want to come for dinner or a beer."

When our food arrived, we discovered the reviews were spot on. Brandy and I each had the house specialty, a seacake. It was similar to a crab cake but with added fish, shrimp, and scallops, all finely chopped and blended together, then fried until it formed a nice crunchy shell with a soft interior. The Caribbean coleslaw was a great side, with papaya, toasted coconut, and pineapple incorporated in it.

"When we get back, I'll tell our cook about these. He could get some ideas from them." It was Brandy talking, not me. I'd promised Cam I'd be a mostly silent partner, but that didn't mean I wouldn't try subtly inspiring a few small changes. I wouldn't be a good partner without pointing out some of what works well for others that might work for us, too.

Over lunch, I told Sandy that I'd read a few of his books.

"Well, make sure you buy the rest of them. I've got a boat and a beer fund to maintain."

I couldn't tell if he was serious or not, so I nodded politely. Then he winked at Brandy, but I still wasn't sure.

For a couple of guys that were so famous, they were totally down to earth, not to mention funny as hell. We could've listened to the two bicker back and forth all day. When we left, they were still bickering over which of them would pay their tab.

Even though the place was crowded, I still hated leaving Mallard Cove. I knew it wouldn't be my last visit. But we had places to go and other people to see. Not to mention, tanning to do at a low speed on the way back to Mobjack Creek.

13

BABS

T *hat evening...*

THIS WAS my second time going with Brandy to the White Horse Bistro, a popular local restaurant. It was so popular that the reservations usually got filled up fast on Fridays and Saturdays. And tonight, we were lucky enough to snag a parking spot on the street, directly opposite the front walkway. I hurried around the Jeep, opening Brandy's door and earning a smile for my effort. She wore dress jeans and that low-cut top she'd talked about, made from sheer white linen. While today was only the first day she had used that tanning accelerator, she was already showing good results. Or rather, that shirt showed off the results, leaving no doubt about her topless tanning.

We were a few minutes early, and the hostess steered us into the bar to wait until our table was ready. As luck would have it, the only open spots at the bar were right next to Babs. Out of the corner of my eye, I saw Brandy suppressing a grin. Babs was wearing the same blouse she'd had on a couple of weeks ago when we were here last.

Just below her cosmetically smoothed neck was that same heavy gold serpentine chain that sported a gold cougar at the bottom. Babs was definitely one who liked to advertise in more than one way.

Her pretty face with the capped white teeth smiled at me from under her long, glossy black mane. That smile waned slightly as she studied Brandy in her new top. She apparently wasn't a fan of competition and wasn't happy that the guy she was with was now staring at Brandy, almost drooling as he did. He was dressed like a used car salesman with a fondness for loud clothes and gaudy gold jewelry, including a huge gold-plated watch.

This wasn't the same gorilla-sized Hispanic man she'd been with the last time we'd seen her. Brandy had said that Babs liked a variety of sexual partners and that she'd been with most of the men who'd been in the bar that night. Brandy had been the head bartender here until the night of the incident with that deputy two years ago. This was the job she'd been coming from when she was attacked. As the bartender, she'd seen Babs in here often with her long list of short-term companions.

"Well, Brandy, new clothes, but same old fellow I see. Are you going to introduce us this time?" This last part was delivered in a syrupy-sweet voice. Brandy had declined to introduce us before, not because she felt threatened but because she simply didn't like Babs and didn't want her to participate in our conversation.

"Ah, Babs. Same old outfit and a new fellow, like always. And no, I'm not." She stepped between Babs and me; her back turned toward her and the car salesman-looking guy, much to his obvious disappointment.

Babs said loudly, "I don't blame you for being afraid of competition."

Brandy started to turn and say something, but I put my hand on her arm. I leaned to my right so that I could look around her and straight at Babs. "Ma'am, I hate to break it to you, but there's no competing with her. Brandy didn't need any surgical help to win, either. True beauty can't be created by using a scalpel."

The shocked look on Babs's face was priceless. Then, the used car guy saw this as an opportunity to show off for his date. "Hey, that's no way to talk to a lady, pal."

"I'm not your pal, and I wasn't talking to my girlfriend. She's the only lady here. So both of you bugger off and mind your own business."

The guy started to move around Babs to get at me, but that's when a big red-haired guy stepped in. "Mike, I've warned you about causing trouble in here. Unless you and Babs want to get banned, you'd be smart to do as Danny said." He turned to us, "I've got your table ready if you two want to follow me."

We went into one of the smaller dining rooms. The White Horse Bistro was in a grand old manor-style house with large two-story white columns on the front slate porch. The interior was like a large home, with its first floor converted into a restaurant. There were only a handful of tables in each room; this gave the place a very intimate feeling.

The red-haired guy was Fred Ayres, the owner of the White Horse and several other restaurants, including the Bay Breeze, a restaurant on Gwynn's Island. He was in a dispute with his landlord over there. The property was owned by the county, which, of course, meant that it was managed by Ted Clifford. Fred sunk well over a hundred grand into the derelict property in return for a lower-than-market rent. Then Ted got elected and tried to evict Fred, who had made the place a smash hit by then. Ted wanted to take the property for himself and planned to put a relative in charge after he controlled it. Last I heard, the whole thing was tied up in court.

Fred motioned me to my chair while holding Brandy's out for her. "I'm sorry about Mike, Danny. He's wanted a shot at Babs for so long and saw a chance to show off."

Brandy frowned. "He better have had all his shots since he wants to screw her."

Fred chuckled slightly. "What can I get to drink for you two?"

We gave him our drink orders, and he went after them.

"I'd say your tanning has paid off."

She smiled. "That was fun. I took crap off that chick for so long when I worked here, and there were limits to what I could say or do to retaliate back then. It feels good not to have to put up with her anymore. And I like what you told Mike."

"Just telling it like it is. Speaking of which, I'm surprised that Fred remembered my name."

"Fred remembers everybody's name. Plus, it's a small town, so he probably knows all about you by now."

"I thought I was keeping a low profile."

She laughed. "Hardly. A motorcycle escort from the Sheriff's Office back to the docks, with the biggest lawyer in the state as your chauffeur? More folks than Fred have heard about you by now. I'm surprised that Babs doesn't already have your name and number."

I grimaced. I wanted nothing to do with Babs besides kidding Brandy about her occasionally. I shook my head, "She's definitely not my type. You, on the other hand..."

"I, on the other hand, had better be!"

"Trust me."

"I don't have any choice since you're headed back to Crozet for a while. You're the only guy I've trusted since...that night."

"I know, and that's not something I take for granted. But I'll only be gone a few days, then I'll be back before you know it. Besides, you'll soon get tired of me and look forward to the times when I'm gone."

"Don't count on it."

Fred returned with our drinks, saying, "These are on me. Sorry for the unpleasantness at the bar, and congratulations on winning round one with Tiny and Ted."

I was surprised. "Thanks, but you didn't need to do that! How did you know about what's going on between me and those two?"

"It's a small town. Congratulations, too, on throwing in with Cam; he's a good guy, and that marina property is beautiful. I'm glad that place won't be turning into condos. I'm also glad that you managed to coax Brandy out and about. She's been a hermit for far too long." He smiled at her.

She returned the smile. "I was waiting for someone who's worth getting out and about with. Cam's lucky to have him as a partner."

Fred's eyebrows shot upward. "That, Danny, is about as high praise as you'll get around here. Brandy is tough to impress."

"She sure impressed me, Fred. But what did you mean by 'round one' with the Cliffords?"

"I mean, those guys don't give up so easily. Like my fight with them over Bay Breeze; I've got a temporary injunction against the County, allowing us to reopen, but Ted's using the taxpayers' money to pay his attorneys to fight me, and I have to come out of pocket. He's always looking for another angle to come at me with and will do the same with you. Watch yourself, and make sure you don't speed around here. Tiny will definitely want to take another shot at you."

"Thanks for the advice. If I can do anything to give you a hand in your fight against the Cliffords, I'd be happy to help."

Fred looked at Brandy. "Looks like you've found a real stand-up guy, Brandy."

She nodded. "He is. He's good for me, and it's good to have him in our area, too."

"Well, you folks enjoy your dinner; I'll send your server right over."

After Fred walked off, I said, "It's more like you are good for me. If dealing with the Cliffords is the price I have to pay to be around here and around you, it's a bargain."

Brandy seemed to be studying my face. "Danny, I want to go visit Crozet with you. Maybe not tomorrow, but soon."

"Ah, you want to come over and meet my wife and kids?"

"That's not close to being funny. No, I want to see the other side of you."

"I'm pretty sure you've seen every square inch of me."

"Smartass. I've seen you adapting to being here at the coast. That shows me what you're like on vacation. I'd like to see what you're like at home when you're working. I want to see where you grew up and the area that helped make you into who you are today."

"We can arrange that. Let me know when you want to come over."

"I was hoping we could ride over and back together sometime."

"Ah, you want to drive Sassy on a long drive."

"No. I mean, yes, but that wasn't where I was going with this. I just want to know more about you. Does that make you nervous?"

"Not much makes me nervous about you. I'll be glad to have you come back with me to Crozet. It's beautiful but in such a different way than this area. I'd love to show you around. Do you have any vacation time coming?"

"Two weeks. I just need to get my shifts covered."

"Didn't you say Sue needed more hours to cover a tax bill?"

"I did, and she does. I'll see if she can take my shifts."

14

GOIN' HOME

T*he next morning...*

I WAS HEADED west in the Jeep, er, make that in Sassy. And I should've said *we* were headed west, as Brandy was in the passenger seat controlling the radio. It turned out that Sue had been very happy to cover for her, and Cam was glad she was finally using some of her vacation time. He'd been worried that she needed the break after two years without using any of it. He knew that once an employee got burned out, getting them back on track was next to impossible, and that was why prevention was so important. I was glad Cam and I were on the same page about this.

After Brandy and I passed safely through Richmond's highway craziness, I started to relax as the traffic thinned a bit. She asked me, "What do you like the most about Crozet?"

"I like that I got to live there before it got wrecked. However, the increased population is a double-edged sword. On one hand, our slow-paced, laid-back lifestyle is history, but on the other hand, a lot of those new people spend money at my brewery. I wish that you'd have gotten to see the town twenty years ago."

"Twenty years ago, I was a year from being old enough to drive yet, Danny. Then again, so were you."

I grinned, "Yeah, but I drove anyway. It was so different back then. We only had one traffic light at the entrance to town. Now we've got four."

"Weren't you scared you'd get caught?"

"The key was to nod and wave at the county cops, not act like you were scared or hiding something. There were only a couple of cops that patrolled the west side of the county, and they weren't out our way very often. You're right; twenty years ago, I was only a year from being able to get my license, and they assumed I must have it already. I was driving this same Jeep back then, though it was pretty ratty before I eventually restored it. The AC didn't work, so I kept the doors off in the summer. It was easy to see in and tell it was me driving.

"The high school had a driver's ed class and used a new rental car with a big 'Student Driver' sign on the top for the road part. It stuck out in traffic. On my last day of driver's ed, we passed one of those cops going the other way. He almost got whiplash when he craned his neck around after recognizing me. Fortunately, he got a call right then and had to respond to it. I took my driver's test the next day and got my license.

"He spotted me a couple of days later and pulled me over. He thought for sure he had me, and boy, was he pissed when I showed him that valid license!"

"Your parents didn't care that you were driving all that time without one?"

This was the hard part of having Brandy come home with me, dredging up some of the more painful past. "My mother took off with some guy when I was in second grade, and after that, it was just my dad and me. He worked on a local farm and was gone from sunrise to sunset. I worked every summer and saved up to buy this used Jeep. I had put a 'Farm Use' tag on it; there were many of those around when we used to raise crops instead of houses. My dad didn't care I was driving without a license so long as I stayed out of any big trouble."

"Do you still see your mom?"

"Not since the day she walked out the door. I have no idea where she is or if she's alive or dead, and I don't care."

"What about your dad?"

"He died in a tractor accident the summer after I graduated from high school. Left me the house and enough life insurance to pay it off, fix up this Jeep, and do the engine swap."

I glanced toward her. "What about your parents? Do you see them a lot?"

"They were killed in a car crash when I was eighteen."

Oh, crap. Emotional landmine. I said, "I'm sorry."

"Nothing for you to be sorry about."

"No, I mean, I'm sorry that I never asked before and that it took you asking about my parents first."

"Again, nothing for you to be sorry about. What's in the past isn't important."

I said, "It is important because it helped shape who you are today. It also explains a lot."

"Like what?"

"Like why you are so independent. Why, since...that incident...at least according to Fred, you've been a 'hermit' and haven't needed anyone else. Though I'm damned if I know how I talked you back out of your shell, especially since I didn't even know you had one."

She was quiet for a minute, obviously thinking. I wasn't going to rush her. "I've been wondering about that myself, but now I think I've figured it out. From the start, I sensed there was something different about you, but I couldn't put my finger on it until now. Both of us were cast out into the world completely alone before we were twenty. No parents and no siblings. Quickly learning how to swim in this world before it could drown us. That probably had a lot to do with our connection."

She reached over and silently took my right hand, which had been resting on the console. I squeezed hers while I stared straight ahead. No words were necessary; saying anything right then would shatter the feeling we were sharing.

Half an hour later, the terrain became noticeably more rolling, and in the distance, we could begin to make out the crest of the Blue Ridge Mountains. Soon, on top of a short mountain on the left, we could see the roofline of Monticello, Thomas Jefferson's home. I pointed it out.

"Jefferson's place. He's buried up there, too. He was the first person to cultivate wine grapes in the New World. Everybody thinks California is the birthplace of American wine, but they're wrong. He kind of has a presidential library, but it's not here. He left all his books to become the nucleus of the Library of Congress up in DC."

"I didn't know all that. We have so much history in Virginia. And what a huge landscape contrast here compared to what we have in Mathews. The hills and the mountains are so beautiful. Must be nice to have both this and the coast now."

I nodded. "The realization of a dream. Reaching a life goal. Though I never thought about buying into a marina before. Life is such a wild ride. You never know what's around the next corner."

Out of the corner of my eye, I saw her look at me and slightly tilt her head. "Or, who." She smiled and squeezed my hand. I squeezed back and nodded.

We got off the interstate, taking the same route as I did before. She loved it when we hit the winding, tree-covered incline part of the road as we got close to the Crozet town limits. I romped on the accelerator.

"This is part of why I put the V8 in Sassy. The old six-cylinder and the two-speed automatic transmission would start to lug as I went up this hill. Now, she eats it for lunch." I grinned as I looked over at Brandy, who was also grinning.

She was amazed when we broke out onto the flatter, open part of the road with the views of the Blue Ridge just past the cornfields and pastures. "I didn't know views like this existed here."

"Neither did that other tourist gal I told you about. Hey!"

I'd gotten a poke in the ribs for that one, though I probably deserved it.

"I'm not just some tourist, you know."

"Believe me, I do," I explained why the left side of the road was lined with developments while the right was still farmed.

She said, "I wish they'd leave it alone."

"That makes two of us."

A couple of minutes later, I pointed out my Moonrise Brewery. Again, I saw Lana working inside, and I honked as we passed. She stopped mid-wave, surprised to see me coming back into town with a woman.

"Looks like you surprised her."

I shook my head. "No, you surprised her."

A minute later, we spotted a burgundy-painted train with a matching engine on the downtown siding. Brandy commented, "Whoa!"

"You can say that again. I've seen a few private cars pulled through town by Amtrak, but never an entire private train, complete with an engine. I wonder why it's parked here?"

She said, "Maybe it has something to do with that tourist train you told me about?"

"Maybe. The same company owns that siding. But as more money flows into our little town, the less strange scenes like this become. I'd give about anything to have things back as they were when I was growing up."

"I'm glad you're helping to keep my part of the state from getting ruined."

"Me, too. I love it down there almost as much as here."

Brandy nodded. "I can understand why now."

A mile later, the train tracks turned toward the Crozet tunnel through Afton Mountain, and farms began reappearing. One of the old farms on the left was nearing the end of its transformation into some hedge fund guy's weekend estate. Landscapers were busy planting trees and shrubs by the road, and a Bentley was pulling out of the driveway.

"That's some of the change you were talking about."

I nodded. "A lot of the workers in those crews are from the other side of the mountain, where houses cost half of what they do here. Like in Mathews, we're getting pushed out of where our families have lived for generations. I don't need to tell you how sad that is."

"Not when I'm living in an old houseboat, you don't."

We passed a few vineyards on the rolling hillside. I said, "More and more pastures are being planted in grapes. They're calling this area 'the Napa of the East Coast.' It has taken a few decades, but Virginia wine is finally getting the respect it deserves."

A few miles later, I turned left into the club's driveway. As we climbed the curvy ribbon of asphalt, we finally came within sight of the buildings.

Brandy commented, "Sure can't see this from the road. This place just screams money. I'd have never thought you owned something like this that day you showed up at the marina."

"Had me pegged as a hobo, did you?" I chuckled.

"Of course not, but I never envisioned this. It's so cool."

We went on around back to the hidden garage. I opened the door and drove in, noting that Parker's Ferrari was already there. I'd hoped she wouldn't be here after that stunt she pulled on Brandy. But I knew they'd have to settle things in person at some point anyway, so maybe sooner would be better than later. Maybe.

Brandy had already spotted the tunnel leading to the blast door, and she looked like a kid getting her first glance at the gates to Disney World.

"This is so cool, Danny!"

"Which is exactly how I felt when I first saw it. C'mon, leave your stuff in the Jeep, and I'll give you a tour of the bomb shelter."

After a quick tour, Brandy shook her head slightly, saying, "You didn't see a fancy hole in the ground; you saw the coolest private poker-playing venue ever."

"Something like that. You know, you can play cards sitting cross-legged on the ground, too. But the best games have an upscale atmosphere with a little mystery. It took a while to figure out that this place could have all those elements, but when I did, it came together nicely."

"I'll say. With its history and atmosphere, I can understand why the DC bigwig players want to join."

I nodded. "Though we're still picky about who we let in."

"Aren't you worried that someone you turn down will turn you in to the authorities?"

"No, for two reasons. If they did, I'd hear about it before any raid might happen. But most of all, they know if they did that, their days of playing in any top-ranked private game anywhere on the East Coast are over. It would be the equivalent of a death sentence to a real player."

We picked up our stuff from the Jeep, and I led Brandy to the long hallway. I dropped off my used linens and clothes in the laundry, then went to my apartment, where she looked around.

"Very...bachelor-ish."

"Are you describing me or my home?"

"Yes."

I laughed. "C'mon into the bedroom; you can put your clothes and stuff in there."

She followed me in, then said she needed to hit the head after the long ride. I retreated into the main room of my apartment to wait for her. There was a knock on my door, and before I could even answer it, Parker walked in.

"Hi Danny, Hitch said he saw you drive in. I've got great news. Nelson Poltz is bringing in a new prospective member today. And get this: the guy travels on his own private train! Poltz said the guy also wants to play in the games."

"Hello to you, too, Parker. Well, you know we have a strict vetting process that'll have to take place before any of this can happen."

"Did you miss the part about him being a pal of Nelson Poltz? We'll need to fast-track him!"

"Again, whoever this guy is, he will have to be vetted, just like your father and every other player here was."

I'd no sooner finished the sentence when Brandy walked into the room. Parker looked like she'd just been hit with a baseball bat.

"What the hell is she doing here?"

Brandy replied, "Well, hello, Parker. Nice to see you with your clothes on."

I said, "Parker, this is my girlfriend, Brandy."

Totally ignoring Brandy, Parker said, "Girlfriend? When the hell did that happen?"

"After that little stunt that you pulled on the phone. Thanks for that, by the way. It made us realize a few things that drew us closer, faster."

Parker's mouth opened and shut, but no sound came out. Without another word, she turned and went out, slamming the door behind her.

Brandy said sweetly, "Gee, was it something I said?"

I rolled my eyes, though I couldn't blame her; Parker had it coming. Now, I needed to talk to Hitch about whoever this guy was that Poltz wanted to bring in.

"C'mon, I'll show you around the rest of the club; then I've got to deal with something."

"I overheard her talking about some Poltz guy?"

"An ultra-wealthy pain-in-my-ass. But still a club member."

"Why keep him?"

"Because he's dead money." When she looked confused, I added, "It means a novice or bad player who loses consistently. The other players like how he runs up the pots, even without a chance of winning. He can't bluff worth a damn, either. Money in the bank for everybody else at the table."

"Got it."

We went out to the dining room, where lunch was starting. I introduced Brandy to Hitch, smiled at some of the members, and then walked through the kitchen to let the "back of house" staff know I cared about and appreciated them. On the way back out, I saw Parker now holding court at the bar with a few of the younger male members fawning over her, undoubtedly hoping for a chance at a last-minute date for tonight. She ignored the two of us, and I was glad.

Hitch was sitting at the end of the bar, watching the dining room and bar patrons. I invited him to join us for lunch in the private dining room. Then, the three of us went in, sat down, and gave our lunch orders to our server.

I asked Hitch, "How was everything while I was gone?"

"You were gone?" He smiled.

"Very funny. Seriously, did you run into any Parker issues?"

He shook his head. "Whatever you said to her changed things; she was pretty mellow."

Brandy snorted. "That chick? Mellow? Ha!"

Hitch looked at her, amused. "Already have a run-in with her, Brandy?"

"Oh, yeah. I don't think she particularly likes me; the feeling is mutual, too."

"She doesn't like any woman who warms up to or gets near Danny."

Now, it was Brandy's turn to look amused, and it was directed at me. "I bet the ol' wife and kids really pissed her off."

Hitch looked confused. "Wife? Kids? Something I don't know about, boss?"

I said, "Figure of speech." I glared at Brandy, who smiled. I was glad she thought this was funny now because it wasn't the other night when I had to drive over to the boat after midnight.

Hitch and Brandy carried most of the conversation over lunch, which was exactly as I'd hoped. They were the two people I was now the closest to, and I wanted them to get to know each other better.

After Brandy excused herself to go to the head, Hitch said, "She is a class act, Danny. Super smart, too."

"I know. There was something about her when we first met."

"I get that. She's tough but easy to talk to and even easier on the eyes."

"Hey! Be careful going down that road."

133

"What? I mean, she's the whole package! I can't comment that she's pretty as well as smart?"

"You can, at least as far as I'm concerned." Brandy was grinning as she walked back into the room.

I said, "We were just..."

"Comparing notes on me. That's fine, I get it; Hitch is your closest friend. I'd be worried if you two didn't discuss me at some point. Do you want me to go out again and come back in a bit?"

I couldn't tell if she was kidding or not about that last part, but Hitch quickly replied, "Nope. I've said all I need to say except that you are also very direct and don't seem to dodge much. I like that. As you've discovered by now, Danny is the same way. Cuts down a lot of time, not having to beat around the bushes."

Brandy agreed. "You're just as direct. Life's too short not to be, Hitch."

"It is, indeed." He looked over at me and nodded. Through our few years together, out of the very short list of women I'd brought to the club, Brandy was the only one who had earned the "Hitch nod of approval." He watched out for me; like Brandy mentioned, he was direct.

I remember one woman I started dating who Hitch despised. It was the first time that he called me "boss." He only did that when he was about to tell me exactly what he thought about something or someone, whether it was a positive or negative comment. He'd done that earlier to let me know this was coming, probably the next time we were alone.

Anyway, after he called me "boss" that first time, he told me that my new woman was bad news. Very bad news, in fact. The worst kind.

"Boss, I know she's probably great in the sack, but that's because she's had a lot of experience...with most of the bar crowd down at Farduners. She keeps moving up the ladder because she's bound and determined to nail down somebody who can get her out of that slum she's living in over in Waynesboro. Looks like she thinks you're her guy."

Farduners was a restaurant and bar frequented by many of the locals. It was on the road into Crozet, right next to the roundabout. I was so mad at Hitch right then that I almost fired him. It would've been the worst decision of my adult life. He was right, of course. That woman was very skilled in the "bedroom arts," skills that come from a lot of practice with a lot of different partners. Skills that could blind a man, causing him to see only what he wanted. Like I was.

Once my bruised ego healed a bit and I started using my big head instead of my small one, I realized he had been right. That woman had a lot of the same "qualities" of Babs. And you know how Brandy got mad at me for buying those additional outfits? This gal would've kept piling them up on the counter for me to buy. Hitch had saved me a small fortune and a truckload of heartache. There was no way that chick would ever be faithful to and satisfied with only one man.

So, I got rid of that woman and moved Hitch up to the manager's job. I knew that no matter what came at us in the future, I could depend on him to "tell me like it is." That was something so rare these days, especially when it was coupled with great management abilities and the ability to keep things in confidence.

"Danny? Hey, Reynolds!" Brandy had apparently been trying to get my attention.

"Hmmm? Oh, sorry. I was thinking…"

"Hitch was saying there's a lot to see here in your little town and that I should check out the Blue Ridge Parkway before I go back home."

"When the man's right, he's right. It's about as different as it gets from Mathews. Definitely something to see. Then there are the wineries, my brewery, and a few unique little shops. It's all on the list of things I want to show you."

"Boss, don't forget Poltz's guest. He's here today and tomorrow, and you'll need to meet with him at some point."

"Yeah, I think tomorrow will be good. Find out the guy's name and give Tripp a call. See what he can find out about the guy before the meeting. The last thing I want to do is go into it and get blindsided."

"Will do."

15

WORKING PARTS

It had been quite a while since I'd been up on the Blue Ridge Parkway and even longer since I'd stopped at the scenic overlook. The view from here to the valley a thousand feet below was stunning. We could see hundreds and hundreds of acres of vineyards, estates, corn and soybean fields, plus numerous cattle and horse farms.

Brandy said, "It's hard to believe this is the same state, Danny. The landscape couldn't be much more different than between here and Mobjack Creek."

She had me get out of the Jeep and stand next to her behind the rock knee wall that protects idiots from getting too close to the dangerously steep cliff edge.

"Contrasts are what makes life interesting. Imagine a day with no night or a night with no day. Or if the whole state was flat. There wouldn't be much of a view from here if it were."

Brandy turned me around and tucked in close to me, using her phone to take a picture with the valley in the background.

"Ah, yes, the obligatory social media selfie," I commented dryly.

She frowned. "No! You know I don't even have a social media account. This is for me to look at when you're here and I'm back at Mobjack Creek."

"I'm hoping there will be fewer and fewer of those days ahead. You've seen how lucky I am to have Hitch to handle things at the club. I'll introduce you to Lana at the brewpub and Luke at the distillery this afternoon. Those two are also why I can spend more time away from here."

Looking down and to the north, we watched as a train came into view far below us. Two engines were pulling a long line of empty coal cars heading for the tunnel through Afton Mountain. I told her how this train would eventually arrive in West Virginia, reloading for the return trip to Lambert's Point terminal in Norfolk, where the coal would then be transferred onto freighters bound for overseas ports. We watched until it disappeared into the mountain.

We drove back toward Crozet, taking the two-lane state road instead of the interstate. After we dropped several hundred feet in altitude, we intercepted the train tracks off to our right. An Amtrak train was also headed east, staying even with us. Then, half a mile later, it crossed overhead on a trestle, switching over to our left side before disappearing around a bend shortly afterward.

"That one seemed to be moving faster than the coal train going the other way," Brandy remarked.

"It was. While it may not seem like it, that passenger train is going downhill, and it's a lot lighter than the coal train. There's a siding on the other side of the mountain they must've been sitting on waiting for the coal train to pass. It looks like that engineer is trying to make up for some lost time; it's a bit later than normal."

WE PARKED in the back at Moonrise, taking the stairs by the loading dock. Brandy looked down the tracks that were so close by, seeing our little downtown in the distance. "Almost looks like the town is here because of the trains."

I shook my head. "The town was already here, but it grew a lot because of the trains. Peaches and apples were then shipped via train, allowing for the expanded production of the local orchards. My building was originally a frozen pie plant; they switched to making

TV dinners when pie production was moved out of state. Since it was set up for food production, it was perfect for the brewery...and other things." I winked at her.

I gave Brandy the nickel tour of the hidden distillery and the brewery, introducing her to Luke before we moved into the bar for a beer. Lana looked Brandy over carefully; she was a bit protective of me. But it didn't take long before the two were chatting like old friends. With each of them running bars and supervising staff, it wasn't that surprising.

Tripp Sanders was hanging out with Bobby at the far end of the concrete-topped rectangular bar. Tripp saw me and then motioned that we needed to talk. I left Brandy and Lana chatting while Tripp and I got up and walked to an empty corner of the room.

"Hitch told me about that guy you want to be checked out, and I'm just getting started. I've got a lot of feelers out, but I can already tell you that you need to be careful with this one. Very careful. The guy is Russian, and I'm already getting bad vibes, just from what I'm finding on the surface.

"I don't want to tell you much more until I have all the facts together, but I can tell you this much: he's got major money. That train on the siding in town is his favorite way to travel. This is despite the fact he's got a Gulfstream 650, too. But he's got a thing for trains. He spends more time riding on that than at any of his properties. And he's got a lot of properties and businesses, both here and in Russia. I'll let you know when I find out more, but like I said, be careful with this one."

"Got it. Thanks, Tripp. The sooner you can find out everything about him the better. I'm going to put off our meeting until tomorrow and give you as much time as I can before it. But I don't know how long the guy is here for."

"I guess we're about to find out."

We went back to our seats at the bar, and I heard a train horn in the distance. I looked at my watch, realizing it was our little tourist train.

I told Brandy, "C'mon, I want to show you something."

We went out through the brewery production room, leaving the big door to the loading dock open. We made it just in time to see the train, with Robby Connors tooting his horn and waving to us. Again, the riders looked out through their windows and into the brewery.

"That is so cool! I'd love to ride on it and go through that tunnel."

"I'll see if we can't make reservations for this fall; that's the best time when the leaves change. And speaking of changing, let's go back to the club and get cleaned up; I've got somewhere special in mind for dinner."

AS WE PASSED the club's parking area, I saw a Cadillac Escalade painted the same color as that train on the siding. This guy was consistent, if nothing else. Hitch had seen us drive in and met us in the hallway outside my apartment. I told Brandy to go in, and I'd be right there.

Hitch said, "Hey, sorry to bug you, Danny, but Poltz wants to meet with you about membership for his friend."

"You told him that can take a while, right?"

"I did, and he wasn't happy. You know, typical Poltz being a prima donna. He wants to meet with you now."

"Yeah, well, that ain't happening. We're in a hurry to get ready for dinner and go out. Tell him that I'll talk to him tomorrow afternoon."

Hitch looked concerned. "I don't think he will be happy about that, Danny."

"I'm not happy about him trying to throw his weight around. Tell him I'm tied up until two tomorrow, and I'll meet with him then. He can take that appointment or leave it."

I could tell Hitch was surprised I was being so rigid and unaccommodating, which was not my usual style. That's when I shared Tripp's warning with him. "So, I want to give Tripp as much time as possible to let him gather information about the guy. But I'm already getting bad vibes from this."

Hitch nodded. "Me, too. I'll pass along that appointment, and we'll see what he says."

I entered my apartment and found Brandy in the bedroom, already stripped down to her bra and panties. She was hovering over the clothes she had brought with her, trying to decide what to wear.

"How dressy is this place tonight?"

"Uh, dressier than what you have on, not that I'm complaining, mind you. But this is Crozet, and you can get away with almost anything...except that. It's not Key West or South Beach."

"Funny. How about jeans and a linen top?"

"Perfect."

I started getting undressed, pulling my belt out of my pants and laying it on my bed. Brandy got a curious look on her face, then came over, picked it up, and examined it. "What's with this buckle? It doesn't want to swivel at all."

I took the belt from her, popped the leather flap loose from a catch behind the buckle, and pulled the attached three-inch knife blade from its hidden sheath.

"This is the last present my dad ever gave me before he was killed. He always told me that a knife was the most valuable tool there is and that I should always carry one. I've never forgotten that." I returned the knife blade to its sheath and put the belt back on the bed.

"I never noticed that before."

I replied, "That's the point; it isn't obvious."

"So, your concealed weapon permit covers it?"

"No, it doesn't need to. The blade is three inches long, which is the maximum length you can legally carry concealed in Virginia. Even Tiny can't do anything about it." I smiled at that thought. It was another thing about me that would irritate the heck out of Tiny if he knew I was carrying it.

Brandy tilted her head slightly as she got lost in thought, watching me as I got undressed. Then, a sly smile appeared on her lips, and she asked, "Danny, have you ever thought about doing things to conserve water here?"

"Where the heck did that come from? We haven't had a drought in this area in years. If you look out beyond my loggia, you'll see that our creek is flowing nicely."

She put both hands around the back of my neck, "Yeah, but a little prevention can help avoid future problems. Just think how much water we could save if we showered together. And you can scrub my back at the same time."

"As tempting as that sounds, we need to get going soon; I want to be where we're going before sunset."

"Then I guess you'll just have to learn how to scrub faster."

THIRTY-FIVE MINUTES LATER, Brandy and I were in the Jeep, speeding down the driveway, headed for town. Uri Aslanov was on the outside patio having a drink and saw us leave. He asked Nelson Poltz, "Is that not Reynolds, the club owner? He who is too busy to talk to us?"

Parker Phipps had walked up behind the pair, intending to introduce herself to Aslanov, and overheard this remark. She said, "He doesn't own nearly as much of the club as he used to. I talked him out of almost half of it."

The Russian looked surprised, since this was news to him. He made a mental note to chastise his DC intelligence operative. Surprisingly, her scouting mission apparently hadn't been as thorough as he'd been led to believe. He could have made a huge mistake without this new information.

"So, you are part owner? Who are you?"

"My name is Parker Phipps."

"Congratulations, Parker Phipps. I had not heard, so is something new, yes?"

"Earlier this week, so, yes. I'm adding to my property portfolio in this area. I own Phipps Estate Vineyards as well."

"Is very interesting. You must join us for dinner, would be very nice conversation. I am interested in joining club. I, too, play poker."

Parker quickly looked around and quietly said, "Not all our members play, nor even know about the games. We have a select group who do, and they desire their privacy." She shot Poltz a warning look for obviously having blabbed, but he was on his third martini and either didn't notice or didn't care.

~

"DANNY, this is beautiful! I wish we had something like this at the Rivah Grill."

The pair were having dinner at Crozet Terrace, an open-air restaurant six floors up in the center of town with a stunning westerly view. The venue overlooked the newest part of Crozet and had a miles-wide panorama of the Blue Ridge Mountains. They were sitting side by side on a cushioned bench behind a table, facing west. They were about five minutes away from the sun setting. Brandy used the camera on her phone to take numerous photos and a video of the spectacular sunset.

Danny had a thoughtful look on his face as he stared off into space. Brandy chuckled. "Replaying your memory of our shower? That built-in bench was certainly handy."

"Hmm? Oh, nope, I was thinking about something else, but now that you mention it..."

"Hah! I bet. So, if not that, what then?"

"Something you just said about how the Rivah Grill could use a similar venue—a raised sunset deck. I wonder if it would draw in more customers."

She nodded. "It's not 'if,' Danny, it's a question of how many. My best guess is a lot." She paused a minute, then said, "So, this is how you built your businesses? Constantly thinking up stuff twenty-four hours per day?"

"Twenty-three and a half. You had my undivided attention in the shower." I winked at her.

"Which I'm very pleased that I did." She paused again, seemingly wrestling with whether or not to say something.

I said, "What?"

"I was just wondering..."

"I can't answer your question if you don't quit wondering and ask it."

"How the hell were you not married or at least with a girlfriend when we met? You're thirty-five, intelligent, straight, all your parts work, and you have several successful businesses. You're not new to town, and everybody here seems to know and like you."

"Just lucky, I guess? All my parts work; you're hilarious. But I was under the impression that I have a girlfriend now."

"Damn right, you do. Now. But why not before? And I'm not talking about Parker."

"I'm ignoring that Parker dig. I've had my share of girlfriends in the past, but you're right; I live my businesses twenty-four-seven. At least, I did up until now, that is. I know many people who have lived this way their whole lives; they keep wanting more. I guess that's human nature. But I'm happy with where I am in life right now. While I wouldn't turn down more business and more income, it's not my main focus anymore. I wouldn't do it unless it were fun.

"Buying *Cohiba* was a life-changing moment for me, as was partnering up with Cam on the marina. It's a great investment and fun. The marina, not my boat. As you know, boats are not a good investment." I laughed after my last sentence, which was a huge understatement, as Brandy knew.

"No, they aren't," she agreed. "You dodged my question, though. Why no girlfriend lately?"

I knew this answer might not be the best thing for our relationship, as it had killed so many others in the past. "I guess the biggest reason is that so many of the women around here were looking more for a husband rather than adventures, and I'm not marriage material. It seemed like most of them wanted someone who worked Monday through Friday, from nine to five. Don't get me wrong, I think that's great, but it's not for me; it's not how I live. Unfortunately, more than one of them thought they could change me, but that wasn't what I was up for."

"For the record, I'm not marriage material either, so don't think that bothers me. And thanks for bringing me along with you to Crozet on this trip. I've learned so much about you today: more about what makes you tick and what kind of people you're drawn to as friends."

"I'm glad you wanted to come. But as you can see, almost

everyone I hang with is also connected to my businesses in one way or another. I have a few more things left to check up on, and then we can go back to Mobjack Creek and maybe take a trip in the boat."

"I'm in no hurry; I'm enjoying it here." She put her head on my shoulder, then curled a hand around my arm. Softly, she said, "You were so easy to fall in love with."

I leaned my head against hers. "So were you. I'm glad you've made me stop and watch a sunset, too—not just once, but twice in the same week. That hasn't happened in quite a while. Years, in fact."

"Same here. Never take one for granted."

My text tone sounded. I sighed and looked at my cell phone. Hitch, with a Parker problem. I knew he was frustrated because he never texted me unless it was really important. Like now.

Brandy asked, "Problem?"

I nodded. "Parker. Siding up to the Russian." I texted her, *You need to steer clear of the Russian and Poltz. I'll explain tomorrow after I know more.*

After a minute, she texted back: *I decide who I do or don't hang out with, and besides, he'll make a great club member.*

Parker, this is business. Don't make me bring your father in on this.

Fine, I'll excuse myself. But you had better have a damn good reason when we meet tomorrow.

URI WAS surprised at the sudden departure of Parker Phipps. He had planned on seducing her after dinner, but now that wouldn't happen. He wished he had gotten a look at the text she had read before making excuses and leaving, at least to see who had sent it. In any case, he was glad she had told him about her fractional ownership. Now, she would have to be added to tomorrow's plan, too. It would be a busy day.

16

HOSTILE TAKEOVER

I woke up when I felt Brandy stirring. Her head was on my chest under a mop of blond hair, and one of her arms lay across me. I began stroking her spine with the fingers of my free arm.

"Mrrrrhph. That's almost as good as your massages." Her muffled voice emanated from somewhere within that blond mop. She moved over off my chest and lay face down on the mattress. One finger pointed at her back. "More."

"My, my, aren't we demanding this morning." I was now using both hands.

She said, "I'm not demanding anything more. Unless you stop."

"Isn't that the same as demanding something?" She couldn't see it, but I was grinning.

"Hush. Rub. Thumbs on the spine. Repeat."

"But you're not demanding."

"Harumph."

To be honest, I would have loved to have had a backrub this morning, too. Plus carbs. Things were a tad hazy. After cocktails and a great dinner at the Crozet Terrace, we'd returned to my apartment, mixed drinks, and sat out on my loggia in the dark, listening to the sound of the water rushing by in the creek. A few late-season lightning bugs flickered above the water and the scrub on the far side. Scattered lights were visible on the mountain range, private houses that were just out of reach of the park. Between drink refills, we'd made out like a couple of high schoolers on the loggia's sofa. Finally, I picked her up, cradled her in my arms, and carried her to bed. After a long night of lovemaking, it was somewhere after three before we finally fell asleep.

Muffled voice: "You're slowing up."

"Sorry. I was thinking about what we're going to do today."

"If you want to go a little lower with this massage, we could maybe pick up where we left off last night, for starters."

"Actually, I was thinking about biscuits and sausage gravy."

She laughed. "That would make an even bigger mess in the sheets."

She rolled over on her back. Even without any makeup and her hair all askew, she was still striking. I looked her up and down.

"What?" she asked.

"Just memorizing what you look like."

"Cheater."

"What!"

"You never finished my massage. No biscuits in bed for you."

"Never intended to eat those in bed. Farduners. They have a great Sunday brunch, and we've slept in until mid-brunch. Time to get moving."

"Does this Farduner place have Bloody Marys?"

"Yep. Mimosas, too."

"I love it when you talk sexy. It's that place by the roundabout, right?"

"Yeah?"

"Dibs on driving Sassy!"

URI SAT at the table in his lounge car, having a late breakfast. His view out the adjacent window was of Route 240, and the shops on the far side of the road. As he sipped his second cup of coffee, he spotted that same Jeep he'd seen leaving the club yesterday. Reynolds was in the passenger seat, and a blond woman was driving; they were headed toward Charlottesville. This reminded Uri that he needed to contact Carol Sanders, aka, Patti Edwards. He dialed her number.

"Hello, Uri."

"You missed something on Reynolds. He sold half of club."

"That's not possible, I did a title search two days before my trip."

"Must have happened after that. I need to know why. I have meeting in three hours; I need current information."

"I'll take care of it, Uri."

"Hurry." He hung up.

UP IN WASHINGTON, DC, Carol frowned. Uri's tone bordered on threatening, not just chastising. She went to her computer screen and began digging. On the State Corporation Commission's website, she found the recent changes to the club ownership, as well as a marina over on the coast that Reynolds purchased part of at that time. Then, on the state's personal property tax list, she found out about the boat. Most importantly, she saw that these transactions and their updates had happened after she'd given her report to Uri. She hoped he wouldn't hold it against her, but he wasn't always the most reasonable man and definitely was as scary as they came.

TWO HOURS LATER...

"You are certain this time?"

"Uri, as I said, these things happened after I met with him, and there is also a reporting lag of a few days. But according to all the online data, this is the most current information."

"So Phipps Properties has forty-nine percent. Parker Phipps."

"She's an officer of the corporation, but the real head of it appears to be Alex Phipps, a big Beltway power player. The same thing with Phipps Estate Vineyards in that county."

Uri snorted. "Parker Phipps says she vas owner."

"Not until her father dies."

"Good to know. I will pay you by Cayman account. Vas good work."

After Uri hung up, Carol Sanders let out a sigh of relief, glad that Uri was no longer irritated with her. He paid well, but he was definitely not someone she wanted to disappoint or anger.

Danny and Brandy sat in Farduners' dining room next to a huge window overlooking a running stream. Brandy asked, "Is that the same stream that flows past the club?"

"Yep. And eventually makes its way down to the Chesapeake. So, some of this water may end up at the marina. Funny to think, isn't it?"

"I guess. We're so far from there." She took another pull off of her Bloody Mary and changed the subject. "If the biscuits and gravy here are as good as this drink, this is quite a find."

"Trust me; we'll be back to feeling human in no time."

"Good, then maybe you won't turn me down again when I proposition you."

"So long as it's after I finish this afternoon's meeting, I won't. But I needed to replenish some liquids and take in these carbohydrates first."

She smiled slyly. "I got turned down for orange juice and gravy; we should've called for delivery."

I laughed. "I'll remember that for next time."

Tripp was watching for me on the club patio when Brandy drove us back. Yeah, she wouldn't surrender the keys, but frankly, I didn't put up a fight. It was kind of nice to be able to enjoy the scenery from the passenger seat. Plus, her wide grin as she tackled the hills made it all worthwhile.

Tripp intercepted us in the hallway outside my office, and all three of us went in and sat around my small meeting table. I liked that he didn't give Brandy a second glance now, with her sitting in on the meeting.

"Okay, this guy is bad, as in, really bad. He has a relationship with the Russian hierarchy and sells them secrets he gets by blackmailing political marks in several countries. It would be very dangerous to have him anywhere near your membership. I suspect he has his hooks firmly into Poltz, and that's how he found out about the club and the games.

"He's very calculating and carefully researches his information marks and the people he plays cards with. He's also one of the biggest customers of that same Cayman Islands law firm we ran into. The one which controls the payments to the credit card account that paid for the travel of 'Patti Edwards.' Looks like she works for him."

I said, "That makes no sense. Twenty grand would be nothing to that guy. Why go to all that trouble and expense to rip me off?"

Tripp shook his head as he answered, "I don't think it was about the money. I think it was about you and seeing how you react to things. That's more along the lines of how he operates."

"But I'm not connected to the government, so I'm not one of his marks. And I don't play in any of the club's poker games because I want to avoid any hint of impropriety. I don't get why he'd need to know that."

"He obviously does. There's something going on here."

"Well, it will have to go on elsewhere because, as far as he's concerned, the club membership is full, and there are no openings."

Tripp commented, "Poltz isn't going to be happy if you turn down his friend."

"Yeah, well, I doubt Poltz would want to drop out to make room for Aslanov."

"Probably not."

I turned to Brandy, who had been sitting quietly in her chair, listening to our conversation. "What do you think, Brandy?"

"I agree with Tripp; whatever this is about, it isn't only twenty thousand dollars. Your Russian guy has something much larger in mind. From what you've told me about your membership, it sounds like a target-rich environment for this guy. I think he wants access to them, and somehow, he will want to manipulate them. That's the missing part: how he plans to accomplish this."

Tripp looked at Brandy approvingly. She had apparently gone up several notches in his estimation. "Exactly. Unfortunately, I don't know how he plans to pull this off. Yet. Meanwhile, it would be a good idea to treat him like a shark. Keep an eye on him, never turn your back to him, and avoid his bite."

I WAS in my office watching the live feed from the security cameras. At exactly two o'clock, Uri walked in through the club's front door, followed by two well-built men who were obviously his security guys. Poltz wasn't with him. I saw Hitch intercept them and then start leading the way back toward the private hallway that led to my office. On one of the screens, I saw Brandy sitting at the bar with Parker approaching her. Normally, that might be cause for concern, but right now, my mind was focused on something else. I shut the screen off, not wanting to be distracted during my meeting.

There was a knock at my door right before Hitch opened it and let Uri in. His guys had apparently stayed out in the hallway. Hitch closed the door, also waiting outside my office, leaving me to talk privately with Uri. The two of us sat in chairs next to a coffee table.

I asked, "Where's Nelson? I guess we need to wait for him."

"Is not coming. I do not need Poltz to speak for me; my English is quite good."

"Yes, it seems to be." *So, where the hell was Poltz*, I wondered.

Uri grunted. "Nelson tells me you hold high-stakes games in bunker."

"Some of the members do get together for a few friendly games every now and then."

"I play in several high-stakes games across country. Is not smart to lie to me. That could become game with high-stakes, too. Not smart, Daniel Reynolds."

"Danny or Dan. I don't answer to Daniel."

"It would seem you just did." His eyes narrowed to slits as he shot me an evil, condescending look.

I drew a deep breath, giving myself a few seconds to compose myself. "Whatever. I'm sorry that Nelson seems to have misled you both on the poker issue as well as on membership. Right now, we have a full complement of members. However, we will add your name to our waiting list." Not that we had one, and not that I'd put him on it if we did.

"Perhaps it was you that was misled, Daniel. I do not want membership. I am going to buy you and your partners out of club."

Okay, that just caught me off guard. "Thanks for your interest, but my club is not for sale."

"Everything is for sale. Just question of price and leverage. You could sell and purchase part of marina you don't yet own."

I really hated getting caught with my pants down, especially twice in two minutes. My turn to take a shot. "I suppose you would then be willing to include that twenty grand your woman stole from me?"

The edges of his mouth curled up slightly. "You do not understand concept of leverage. What did you gain by telling me that? Nothing! You have much to learn, Daniel."

"And you have much to learn, Aslanov. Like how using the wrong name over and over just got you thrown off my property and permanently banned from returning. Now get the hell out of my office!" I stood up and pointed at the door.

Uri remained seated, tilted his head slightly, and said as he wagged a finger at me, "You have balls, Reynolds. If you do not want them removed with rusty knife, you will learn quickly to treat me with respect. I will give you free lesson in leverage today, and once you learn, you will want to give me respect."

Uri stood up and went out into the hallway without looking back, closing the door behind him as he did. Suddenly, I felt dread in the pit of my stomach. I called Hitch on my cell, but he didn't answer, which was unlike him. He had his phone on him at all hours and always dumped any other calls in order to take mine.

I entered the deserted hallway and walked to the bar and dining room. I didn't see Hitch anywhere. The bartender on duty recalled Hitch heading for the hallway door with some big guy a few minutes ago but couldn't recall when Parker or Brandy left or in which direction they went.

I retraced my steps down the hallway and checked my office and my apartment, but no Hitch, Brandy, or Parker. I went into the laundry and almost tripped over Hitch's prone body. One side of his head was bloody, and he was moaning. At least he was still alive. I bent over him as he came to, more or less. I grabbed a clean bar towel from the shelf, folded it, and held it against his head to stop any more bleeding.

"Bastard hit me from behind."

"Who?"

"One of Uri's bodyguards. I saw the other one going down the hall behind Parker and Brandy."

That dread in the pit of my stomach just tripled in size. I called Brandy's phone, but it went straight to voicemail. Same with Parker's. Hitch could tell what was happening from the look on my face.

"The garage. That's where they were headed, Danny." Hitch tried to get up but was too wobbly to stand.

"Sit back down on the floor, Hitch. I'll call an ambulance."

"I don't need a damn ambulance, Danny, I need some payback instead."

"Stay down; I'm going to check the garage."

He started to argue, but by then, I was already back in the hallway. Once inside the garage, I saw two smashed cell phones behind Parker's Ferrari. The driver's side visor was flipped down, and the door opener was missing. Parker hadn't yet had it coded into the car's opener console.

There wasn't a soul in the garage, but just to be safe, I checked the bunker. Nothing. I ran back to the laundry, where I found Hitch standing up but holding onto the doorframe to steady himself. He looked hopefully at me, but I shook my head.

"They're not there. He took them. That goddamned Uri took them!"

Just then, my phone rang. A video call. I answered it and saw Uri's face on my screen.

"Daniel, I told you I vould give you lesson in leverage, did I not? Here is first part." The camera turned around, and in what was obviously a lavishly decorated train car, Brandy and Parker were seated on an expensive-looking couch, their hands, legs, and mouths wrapped in duct tape. One of Uri's goons was holding a semi-automatic pistol with a silencer to Brandy's head. Then the camera turned back around, and I was facing Uri again.

"Goddamn you, if you hurt one hair on either of their heads, so help me..."

"QUIET! You are failing lesson already. You must learn when you lose leverage, you must do as you are told. Get in Jeep and drive to my train in Crozet. Do not call police, and come alone. If you try tricks, they die. You have ten minutes. In eleven minutes, one vill be shot. At twelve minutes, they are both dead. Understood?"

"Let them go! They don't have any part in whatever this is."

Uri smiled. "Is hostile takeover." He laughed, and then his face became serious again. "You now have nine minutes."

17

TRAIN RIDES

I drove like a madman, like my own life depended on it because I believed Uri would carry out his threats. I made it to the train in seven minutes, pulling up just as the color-matching Escalade was loaded into an enclosed freight car. The car ramp began retracting into a slot under the door. Apparently, they were preparing to depart.

One of Uri's goons approached my Jeep, motioning me around to the front, where he spun and frisked me. I had anticipated this and had left my pistol in the armored center console of the Jeep. However, he did relieve me of my phone and the folding knife I'd deliberately left in my pocket, intending for it to be found. The idea was to make them feel overconfident and secure. Then the goon spun me around and shoved me toward the boarding steps. I climbed aboard, and he followed close behind, shoving me through the doorway of Aslanov's lounge car after I reached the landing.

Uri was seated in a chair at the far end of the room, which was decorated like a very plush living room. Across from him were Brandy and Parker, still taped up but seemingly otherwise unharmed. The goon behind me now had a silenced semi-automatic pistol in his hand that he'd pulled from his waistband.

Uri said, "Welcome to leverage class, Daniel. Is lesson two. Sit down." He pointed to a spot on the couch next to Brandy. As I sat, he turned to my goon escort. "Vas he armed?"

"He had this." The man held out my Buck knife.

Uri grunted. "Old American sayink: 'You bring knife to gunfight.' Not smart, Daniel."

The train jerked slightly as we began moving westward. Uri's guy remained standing without flinching, obviously used to the train's movement.

I said, "I didn't come here to fight; I only came to get my friends back. Okay, you have the leverage; I'll admit it. What do you want in exchange for their freedom?"

"I told you vat I want: your club. You and Phipps must sign over to me."

"I don't even know how much I'd want for it."

"Here is what I am offerink; your friends' lives. You vill be put off train in Staunton. Then, you vill contact Phipps and arrange for legal transfer of property. We are headed for siding at Greenbrier in Vest Virginia. Once transfer is complete, your friends vill be released there."

There was no way in hell I was leaving Brandy and Parker on this train with Uri since I seriously doubted they would ever be released unharmed. From what Tripp had said, I figured he would probably want to have Alex and me killed after the transfer, too. This guy was a pro; he'd leave no loose ends hanging around for someone to follow and negate the sale.

The train was slowly gathering speed as we passed those old, smaller homes built for the factory workers. I estimated we had less than ten minutes until we would enter the Crozet tunnel. I had the beginning stages of a plan forming in my brain. But I needed to stall in the meantime.

"Why do you want my club so badly?"

"You have interesting membership."

"You've gone to all this trouble just to meet the members? Why not just have Poltz bring you to the monthly member barbeques?"

"If I own club, I control membership. That simple. Not something I can do as guest."

"Control them? How?"

The evil grin reappeared as Uri pressed a hidden button under a side table. A varnished panel under a window slid open, revealing a hidden bookcase filled with DVDs, each marked with a person's name. I could only imagine what was contained in each of them.

"You think your Congress does as it pleases? Nyet. Not vithout guidance. Leverage, Daniel, leverage. More valuable than any currency. I have placed vimmen vith two members of Congress, but vith club, I can access even more."

Yeah, there's no way the women are not coming off this train with me. I just need the temporary darkness of the tunnel for cover. I looked over at Brandy. She had that same look she got when she saw Tiny—kind of a frozen-faced fear. Looking beyond her at Parker, tears had destroyed her mascara, which was running down her face in streaks. I wished I had seen anger on each of their faces instead. But at least Parker wasn't panicking. Not yet, anyway. My job is to keep that from happening long enough for us to be able to get away. Brandy looked at me, and I winked, then she appeared to relax slightly.

I looked at my watch and saw it was twenty minutes from the usual time for the tourist train to pass through Crozet. This meant we would have to pass it, or it would have to pass us, which is what I was counting on. Just beyond the tunnel was a siding; with any luck, we would get to it first. We would then have to pull onto it and let the other train have the main track. Now, we just needed a little bit of luck to come through for us. I saw out the window that we were now crossing that trestle we'd seen on our way down the mountain. The tunnel entrance wasn't far.

Uri had been talking all the while I was formulating my plan. I hadn't listened to his little speech, but I noticed he was now staring more intently at me.

"So, you vill do vat I tell you. Do you understand, Daniel?" For the first time, there was just a small hint of concern in his voice. I needed him to be relaxed and confident in his plan in order for mine to work.

"Yeah, yeah, I hear you."

"If you do not do as I say, or call police, you vill never see your friends in one piece again. Do what I tell you. Is no place you can hide that I cannot find you." He motioned to the case filled with DVDs. The implied meaning was these all represented more leverage. For all I knew, he might even have influence over someone in the Justice Department. I believed he meant every word he was saying.

Uri motioned to his goon that he was to move to my end of the couch. Maybe he sensed a growing threat from me, or maybe it was because I was the only one of the three on the couch who wasn't secured with duct tape. Again, I needed Uri to lower his guard a bit. The goon took up a position next to me, holding that silenced pistol a couple of feet away from my head. That's when things started to go dark. We'd reached the tunnel entrance. At the same time, our train began to slow, apparently in anticipation of switching to the siding soon after we emerged. Fortunately, no one had turned on the car's interior lights.

The combination of darkness and the forward inertia from the braking did manage to catch Uri's guy off guard. At least enough for him to take his eyes off me for a second. I reached down, unbuckled my belt, and undid the catch on the back. In the center of the tunnel, at the peak of the darkness, I pulled the buckle knife from its sheath.

With one hand, I reached up and grabbed the silencer on the goon's gun, forcing him to aim upward. He managed to get two shots off before I was able to drive my knife blade into his side, stabbing him repeatedly and causing him to relinquish his hold on the pistol. He had to use both hands now to try and fend off my attack, grabbing the arm of the hand with the knife. I swung the pistol by the silencer, the butt of the handle connecting with the guy's temple which seemed to dent. He fell to the floor in a crumpled heap, out cold. In the now increasing daylight, I could see he was already leaking red stuff onto Uri's carpet.

The two muzzle flashes had caught Uri by surprise, and he began shouting in a stream of Russian, most of which I'm sure wasn't ready for prime time. I felt like matching him in English since I'd grabbed the pistol close to the end of the silencer, and the edge of my hand got burned by the blowback from the muzzle flash.

As I was turning the gun around to get the grip in my hand, Uri dove over to our side of the car. Not to get at us but into an apparent safe room. A wall section had opened, and Uri was going for the opening it created. As he dove into it, I let off two rounds, but I'd only managed to hit that open door in the semi-darkness. It was now swinging back to its closed position.

I knew that Uri had at least one other henchman aboard the train, and chances were there were several more. The car was getting much brighter as we emerged from the tunnel and began switching to the siding. I took my knife and cut the tape on Brandy's hands and legs, then did the same for Parker, leaving the women to tackle the task of removing the tape from their faces and hair. It was better they pulled their own hair than having me do it.

I bent over the unconscious goon, pulling both my folding knife and my phone from his pocket. Then I went over to Uri's DVD collection and grabbed three, including one whose name on the label I recognized, and stuffed them into my waistband. Then I asked the two women, "Can you guys run?" They both nodded while still pulling off their tapes. "Good, because we're running out of time. Let's go; he's probably already calling in his reinforcements from in there." I motioned to the area where Uri had disappeared.

We made our way out of the same entrance that I came in. The train was still moving slightly, and the drop from the platform down to the gravel was several feet. Not that we had any choice; we'd have to chance a twisted ankle or two. But our luck was holding, and the three of us got to the ground unscathed. We were about two hundred yards away from the tunnel entrance, but that wasn't where I was heading.

"Follow me! We'll jump that fence." I pointed to a fence that lined the tracks by the tunnel.

"Where are we going," Parker whined.

"Shut up and follow Danny," Brandy replied.

"Who died and made you queen?"

I said, "Parker, shut the hell up and follow me. Or, stay here and get shot, your call. C'mon, Brandy." I crossed the main line tracks and climbed over the six-foot-high black powder-coated fence, dropping down next to an asphalt trail. Brandy was two seconds behind me, and Parker was right behind her. We started sprinting for the tunnel, the original one that was now part of the Rails to Trails system.

As we entered the dark and narrow tunnel, the smooth gravel dust surface that covered the old, coarse gravel of the railway gave us great footing. This was important because a hundred yards in, it got very dark. This was why signs at either end warned people to bring flashlights. While we didn't have any, that was fine with me since their light would have given away our position to any pursuers. I knew how tough Brandy was, and she stayed right with me. But Parker surprised me, keeping up with both of us. Fortunately, she had shut up, at least for now.

By focusing on the round circle of light at the other end of the tunnel, we managed to stay in the center of the path and not come in contact with the roughly hewn granite walls. However, at one point, a couple of people strolling side by side yelled at us, telling us to quit running without flashlights and that it was dangerous. If I hadn't been so winded from running, I'd have "commented" on their "gift" for explaining the obvious.

Breaking out into the sunshine at the other end, I stopped for a minute to catch my breath. A train horn echoing through the new tunnel spurred me on. I began climbing over a fence that was identical to the one we'd climbed on the other side of the mountain.

Parker protested. "What the hell are you doing, Danny? We're safe now."

From my perch on the top of the fence, I replied, "No, we're not. They'll have figured out what we did, and they'll be right behind us. You can stay here and wait on them, but Brandy and I are going to hitch a ride."

"On what?"

"Trust him, and come on!" Brandy was reaching the end of her rope with Parker, who reluctantly began to climb.

I stood in the middle of the tracks, checking that the pistol and the DVDs were still secure in my waistband and covered with my shirt. Now, about three hundred yards from the tunnel entrance, I could see the oncoming train's headlight back in the tunnel. There were two things I was counting on; one was Robby Connors spotting me, and two, that he'd be going slow enough through the tunnel to be able to stop for us.

Parker was on one side of me, and Brandy was on the other as we all began waving like crazy. As soon as the engine cleared the tunnel, it began sounding its horn like crazy. We didn't budge. I heard the brakes before I spotted the sparks on the tracks as the big powerhouse dragged its few cars to a halt.

Robby came out on the catwalk, yelling at us "crazy sumbitches" until he recognized me. I climbed up the side ladder with the women right behind me, explaining to Robby that it was an emergency. Suddenly, sparks flew off of the handrail next to me.

"Jesus, Danny, somebody's shootin' at us! Quick, y'all get in the cab."

As soon as we shut the steel door, Robby began accelerating. I looked out the rear-facing window and watched as one of Uri's men climbed over the fence and raced after us. He nearly caught up with the last car before he stumbled and did a faceplant in the old wood ties and gravel. I figured he was now a candidate for stitches, if not for some plastic surgery. Couldn't have happened to a better guy.

Robby took out his phone and was preparing to call the police when I intervened. Over the noise of the engine, I said loudly, "Robby, don't call anybody."

Robby looked at me like I'd lost my senses. "That guy shot at us! I want to give the cops his description."

"Believe me when I tell you, the cops can't touch that guy. Don't worry, we'll handle it."

"What do you mean they can't? How the hell are you going to handle it? You're crazy! That guy came within inches of killing me!"

"You just have to trust me. Do what I say, and you'll drink for free at Moonrise for a year. I need you to stay quiet about the shooting and to drop us off at the Crozet siding."

Robby stared at me like I had a third eye in the center of my forehead. Finally, I saw him start to mull over my offer.

"Throw in bar food, too?"

"Done!"

He shook his head, "You're still crazy, but okay, I'll do it."

I texted Alex, warning him that he's probably been targeted and that he needs to get some security coverage. I said I'd call and explain further in a half hour. Then I texted Tripp and Hitch, saying we were okay and that I'd call each of them soon with more details, but meanwhile, we needed to step up security at the club. I added that if Poltz showed up, they needed to keep an eye on him as well. Then I texted Lana, setting up what I promised Robby.

Over the engine's noise, Parker said in my ear, "Danny, I'll need a ride to the club; I want to pick up my car."

I nodded, even though I had no intention of going back to the club. That is the first place that Uri's guys would look. Then Brandy moved up next to me and wrapped her arms around me.

She said, "Thank you for rescuing us. I kept trying to come up with a plan, but I wasn't having any luck. I knew that he was never going to let us go. This is twice now that you've jumped in to save me."

I wanted to downplay the moment, taking the serious edge off things. "Saving damsels in distress is a specialty of mine. But tell you what, you buy the next dinner at the White Horse, and we'll call it even."

She kissed me at first in reply. "I'm planning on doing more than that."

As much as I wanted to let my imagination run away with that statement, I first needed a new plan for keeping the three of us safe. Unfortunately, I knew that meant Parker was in it with us for the long haul, which wasn't something I really wanted to happen. And if I wasn't thrilled about it, I knew Parker would absolutely hate it.

~

URI HEARD THE THREE KNOCKS, followed by one knock, the "all clear" signal. He opened the safe room door, but in one hand, he held a silenced semi-auto pistol, just to be on the safe side. There were three of his security guys in the train car, not counting the dead one who had bled out on the floor. He'd also been the one who had missed the knife that finished him off.

"Vat about Reynolds and the women?"

The head of security hung his head slightly. "They escaped. Somehow, they managed to stop and board that sightseeing train's engine. I shot at him, but I missed. I'm sorry, Mr. Aslanov."

Enraged, Uri started kicking the body of the now-dead security guy. Spewing a torrent of Russian, the other men in the car began moving away from Uri lest they become the next outlet of his anger.

Finally, Uri stopped and said, "Be glad you did not kill him or Phipps girl. Get us quickly to vhere ve can unload car. Ve need to hunt those three down now. I vant them captured alive!"

Uri saw that his DVD collection had been disturbed. He began picking up the spilled ones and putting them all back in alphabetical order. That's how he knew which three were gone. One of them was his most valuable piece of leverage, and he began cursing in Russian again. He pulled out his phone and dialed Poltz.

"Yes, Uri?"

"Are you at club?"

"I'm pulling in as we speak."

"Go to siding in Crozet; Reynolds left Jeep there. Vhen he picks up, follow him—I need to know vhere it is he goes."

"I could wait here for him..."

Uri exploded again. "Nyet! Do as I say, or I put your video on social media! Now, go!" He hung up, glaring at his head of security again. "Vhy are we not moving? Must I do all myself? Ve need go! Now!"

18

EXODUS

We hopped off the train at the Crozet siding and loaded into my Jeep. I put the DVDs, along with the silenced pistol I'd taken off Uri's goon, into the armored console next to my Glock. As we pulled out onto Route 240, I turned east.

Parker said, "Hey! The club is in the other direction, Danny! I just want to pick up my car and go home."

I said, "Yeah, those are the first two places Uri's crew will look for us. No, we're going somewhere they aren't familiar with."

"Where's that?"

Brandy had already figured it out. "Our marina on Mobjack Creek."

Parker looked horrified. "Where? I've never even heard of Mobjack Creek."

Brandy gave her a fake smile. "That's the whole point, Parker."

Parker frowned, "What is this 'our marina' bit? Are you invested in it, too?"

"No, but I live and work there. I bartend and handle all the servers, too."

"What? You're a waitress? Danny, do you mean to tell me you chose some *waitress* over *me*? Have you lost your mind?"

"No, Parker, I'm completely clearheaded. I did not choose a *waitress* over you; I was lucky enough to connect with one of the most brave and clever women I've ever met. One with great taste in cigars and who knows all about your Stella Starr dress thing."

Both women said simultaneously, "McCartney."

I said, "Yeah, whatever. My point is that she knows a lot about... things. Including things that we both like."

Parker smirked. "Yeah, I'll bet I know what they are, and they aren't clothes or cigars."

I'd had enough. "Knock it off, Parker! Do you really want to know why I was never attracted to you? This! You treat people badly and only see them for what they do, their net worth, or what they can do for you. The point is, you never see them for who they really are. You're missing out on so many of the best people this world has to offer.

"If you knew her, you'd realize that Brandy is just as beautiful on the inside as she is on the outside, something you lack. She doesn't need fancy clothes to be that way, either. On the other hand, you need to disguise your insecurity with a designer this or a designer that, and you try to impress people with your Ferrari. If you were a better person, you'd feel more secure. Then you wouldn't need all that crap to attract people, and you might find a better class of friends."

In the mirror, I saw she was about to go ballistic. "If you're quite finished with this dumb lecture and your ten-cent psychoanalysis, pull over and let me out; I'll call a rideshare to take me back to the club."

Brandy jumped in, probably because she knew Parker wouldn't listen to me now. "Parker, use your head! You know it's not safe to go back to the club or even to Crozet. We're safer sticking together down at the coast. All of us, including you."

I added, "Especially since I'm pretty certain we're being followed. Don't look, but there's an electric Mercedes SUV two cars back, and it's been following us from over by the siding in Crozet. I'm pretty sure it's Poltz."

"You're just trying to scare me so I'll agree to stay with you two."

Brandy shook her head emphatically, "No, Danny's trying to keep you alive. To keep all of us alive. And since you know for certain where we plan to hole up, we can't take the chance on your getting caught and confirming the location. We've already seen what they're capable of; do you doubt they'd hesitate to torture you for that information? Uri screwed up by telling us too much. That's why I know he planned on killing us all along; he got too overconfident. Now, he has to find and kill us to make certain we don't talk about his little video collection and where he keeps it. To prevent that, we'll need to lose our tail, and as much as I hate to say it, you need to stick with us, too."

I smiled, then looked at Parker in the rearview mirror. "What do you think of my 'waitress' now? I told you she was smart. Never underestimate people, Parker. Not to harp on a sore point, but you said you thought Aslanov would be a great new club member. Stop, listen, and learn. Let your prejudices and preconceptions go."

Parker crossed her arms and sat back in her seat. She was resigned now to sticking with us but was still unhappy about it.

I called Alex on speakerphone, giving him a quick rundown of what had happened and where we were headed.

"Is Parker all right?"

"She's fine..."

"Give me that!" Parker yanked the phone out of my hand. "Daddy, Danny won't let me out of the car! He's kidnapping me, and I'm pretty sure he killed a guy back on that train..."

"Parker! Hush up and listen to me. You do everything Danny tells you to do. Until we stop the Russian, you'll be the safest with him."

"You've got to be kidding me, Daddy. Do something and get me out of this!"

"I am, damn it, I'm trying to save your ass! Now, shut up, do as I say, and put Danny back on the phone."

A red-faced Parker passed the phone back to me. Apparently, this was the only time her father had ever cursed at her. I considered it a good start, but he had a lot of ground to cover to make up for her overly spoiled upbringing. The world had yet to give her a good swift kick in the ass, and that was what it would undoubtedly take if she were going to become a decent human being that was worth being around.

"Hey, Alex. You need to get somewhere and hole up as well."

"I already figured that out. If he has as big a network around DC as I've been hearing, it isn't safe for me around here. Until he's taken care of, I need to stay out of sight. So, I'm going to join you down at the coast."

"Good. Another set of eyes to watch our backs will be helpful. I'll text you the address."

"I'll see you in a few hours."

NELSON POLTZ HAD BEEN careful to keep a car or two between his car and the Jeep. It was actually fun at first, a little like something out of a detective movie. He hadn't realized how far they would be going, though. When he'd left Crozet, he had over eighty miles of range remaining on this battery charge. He'd assumed Reynolds was going somewhere close, but then he got onto I-64, heading east. Now, even with the battery regeneration happening on the downhills, he was quickly eating up that charge.

By the time he reached the point where I-64 and I-95 merged in Richmond, the road had flattened out quite a bit. But miles were still miles, and the percentage of charge remaining had almost dropped into single digits. As he passed where I-95 and I-64 split apart, he dropped to eight percent, and the display went from green to yellow. He had never run his battery down this far, and the color change freaked him out. He knew there was a fast charge station not far ahead at Mechanicsville, and he decided to call Uri and tell him he was breaking off his "tail" to go and recharge.

Because Poltz didn't speak Russian, he had no idea exactly what Uri was saying or, rather, shouting. But with the volume and emphasis, he didn't really need a translation; he had a pretty good idea of what it was.

"Uri, I can't change physics! A charge can only take you so far."

"How long vill this charging take?"

"It's a fast charger, so probably forty-five minutes."

More high-volume, rapid-fire Russian came out of the car's speaker.

"Uri, I can't help it! I'm down to eight percent; I've got to charge up."

"You still have charge, and you are stopping? Nyet! Keep going until Reynolds stops or car quits."

Poltz had heard horror stories about what happens when you run completely out of electricity. The windows don't work, the car slows to a stop, then automatically goes into park.

"I can't Uri! I don't want to get stranded out here. It'll be all woods on both sides in a few miles."

"You vould be better off in voods. If you quit and lose Reynolds, you can be latest Internet porn sensation vith your little boys. Or you can keep going until Reynolds stops or you run out of battery. Is up to you."

Poltz swallowed. There was no choice. The obvious age of some of those boys on the videos would send him to prison for a very long time if he even survived behind bars. Pedophiles generally had short life spans in prison. He sighed.

"I'll keep going."

"See? Is not hard decision. Call me vith update."

After Uri hung up, Poltz glanced at the screen again. Seven percent. Several miles later, they turned off onto Route 33, and Poltz was now down to a single car between himself and the Jeep. Traffic had dropped considerably, and so had his battery charge, which had now fallen to three percent. The numbers had switched from yellow to red, and a new message appeared on the screen: *Charging station range warning!* This wasn't good.

Two miles from West Point, the number went to zero. Poltz was now on the verge of panic. He knew West Point was large enough to have a charging station; he hoped he had enough charge remaining to find it. Then, his car began to slow on its own, reacting sluggishly to the accelerator. Just ahead was a high and wide bridge spanning the Pamunkey River. West Point was at the base of the bridge on the far side.

He reached the bridge, but as he started up the incline, the screen went black, and the car slowed further. He pulled over into the wide bike lane, and he could see the taillights of the Jeep disappear over the crest of the bridge in the growing dusk as his own car died. He was furious with Uri but scared at the same time. This wasn't going to be a fun phone call.

~

As we crossed the Pamunkey River, I watched the headlights of Poltz's car peek out from behind the car that separated us. He seemed to be falling behind. Now, pulling all the way over, I saw him stop and the headlights extinguish.

I laughed. "Son of a bitch!"

Brandy asked, "What?"

I patted Sassy's dash cover. "Looks like Poltz's car just ran out of juice. He must not have had a full charge. Yet another reason I love these small-block engine conversions is their range!"

"So, we're safe now?" Parker asked.

Brandy replied, "I wouldn't count on it. If he was reporting back to Uri, and you can bet he was, the Russian now knows which direction we are headed and probably exactly where we're going."

"Which direction we're going, yes, but where we're going? How?" Parker was doubtful.

I said, "He does his research. He mentioned the marina in our meeting. But it's still unfamiliar territory to him, and we have a secret weapon."

Brandy looked surprised. "We do?"

I nodded, then turned to look at her. "Tiny."

. . .

It was dark when we reached Mathews. I went a few miles under the speed limit, just in case. I spotted a sheriff's cruiser sitting with no lights burning down a side street in the middle of town, running radar on a lazy Sunday night with little traffic.

Ten minutes later, we reached the marina. I pulled the DVDs and the two pistols out of the console, handing the silenced gun to Brandy and keeping the other for myself. Being Sunday night, I saw the bar and restaurant were already closed as we passed by.

"You traded out shares in the club to buy into *this*?" Parker made it sound like the marina was something she'd scrape off the bottom of her shoe.

"Wait until you see it in the daylight," I said. "It's so tranquil and serene."

"In other words, dead. What's next? Are you going to move into one of those little tarpaper shacks across from the railroad tracks back in Crozet?"

"I grew up in one of those, Parker. It was our family home and became the first piece of real estate I ever owned. My father left it to me when he was killed."

"Oh."

No apology, just "Oh."

We made the turn from the main dock, watching carefully for any of Uri's people who might have beaten us here. Fortunately, the dock was deserted, most of the boaters having returned home after the weekend. When we stopped behind *Cohiba*, once again, Parker's nose turned up like she'd smelled something bad.

"What?" I asked.

"Nothing."

"Nothing? *Nothing*? You don't have the guts to say what you're obviously thinking?"

"Well, when you said you bought a cabin boat, I was picturing something...larger. I mean, the boats I go out on down in Palm Beach are so much longer."

Brandy had had enough and came to my defense once again in her own special way. "Danny doesn't need to compensate for any...

shortcomings...like so many go-fast boat owners with the loud exhausts or triple or quadruple outboards." I guess Brandy figured that those might be the types of boats Parker liked down in Florida. From the reaction she got, it looked like she'd hit a bull's-eye. "Besides, this boat is the perfect size to handle when it's just the two of us aboard. Which is the way I like it."

"Yes, well, it looks like it's going to be tight for four of us."

"Oh, that's not an issue. You and your father can stay aboard *Cohiba* while Danny and I stay on my houseboat. It has a larger bed, and we like plenty of room."

I realized I needed to do something quickly before this war of words escalated. "Let's get off the dock; I feel kind of exposed out here."

Brandy couldn't resist one more shot. "You can expose yourself all you want over on my boat."

I recalled that video call that Parker intercepted and thought: *Paybacks are such a bitch, eh, Parker?*

Once aboard *Cohiba*, we shut all the curtains and cranked up the AC. Parker looked around at the accommodations, clearly unhappy.

"So, can we go out to dinner now? I'm hungry," Parker said.

I replied, "There are some frozen burritos in the little freezer; you can nuke one of those. We're all going to stay here, out of sight. Your father should be here soon, too."

From the look she shot me, I guess frozen burritos ranked right up there with our marina and my boat. Alex was a good friend and a great businessman, but he didn't know crap about raising a daughter.

Suddenly, I had an idea about how to take the safety off our "secret weapon." I found the Faraday bag and pulled out my old smartphone. Luckily, unlike Poltz's car, it still had a charge. I dialed Hitch.

"Danny? I thought you said this phone..."

I interrupted him, "Yeah, I wanted to call and check on you after the Russians attacked you. I'm pretty sure they're now on their way here to Mobjack Creek and that they're heavily armed."

"I'm fine, but have you called the cops?"

"You didn't because you knew what might happen. And I'm supposed to tell them what, exactly? That I think these guys are spies, and they might be coming to kill me? The cops would ship me off to a psych ward. No, they wouldn't believe me unless I was bleeding or dying. Can't say I could blame them."

"Wow. Well, watch yourself. These guys don't play, and they hate cops. They definitely won't hesitate to shoot you or hurt anyone who gets in their way so that they can."

I thought, *Nice touch about the cops, Hitch. Now, if only Tiny's people are still listening.*

"Roger that. Get better, buddy."

19

SHOWDOWN

Alex showed up a half hour later, bearing gifts. Or, rather, food. A pile of sandwiches from Parker's favorite Northern Virginia delicatessen.

"I wasn't sure how many of us would be here, or how long we would be staying, so I made sure to bring plenty."

I didn't know whether to be mad because he took the risk of stopping or grateful since we were all starving. The burritos were still sitting in their frozen habitat. Then, the aroma of those sandwiches hit me, and my choice was made. Grateful. I knew there was more behind those sandwiches, though. Parker had lit up like a neon sign upon seeing the logo on the bags. Alex had yelled at her for the first time, and this was a silent but delicious apology. I doubted he'd ever stop spoiling her.

～

"Sheriff, you gotta listen to this!" The deputy in the dispatcher's office replayed Danny's conversation with Hitch.

Tiny's forehead furrowed. "Russian spies, huh? I knew there was somethin' off with that fella. Biker gang, hotshot lawyer, an' a pile ah cash; now it all makes sense. He's involved with spies."

"Sounds more like they're after him instead of being involved," the dispatcher commented.

"Ain't you never heard there's no honor among thieves, son? This is some kinda partnership quarrel. And now, I'm gonna grab them Russians an' get the evidence I need ta lock that Reynolds boy away for life!"

"Sheriff, don't you think it's funny that we haven't heard anything off of this phone for days, then all of a sudden, it comes back online?"

"Nah. He probably forgot an' left it on his boat last time an' just found it when he got back."

"I guess so." The dispatcher wasn't convinced.

"I ain't guessin', son. Keep yer damn ears open, an' let me know if ya hear anythin' more."

Tiny called his chief deputy. "Meet me at the turnoff ta Mobjack Creek Marina. Don't put out anythin' on the radio that can be picked up onna scanner." He went on to tell the deputy about the phone call. "We gonna bag us some Russians, and get that damn Reynolds all at one shot!"

I sat in my elevated helm chair in the darkness, looking across the water at the parking lot and the closed bar while eating one of the best sandwiches I'd had this year—maybe of this decade. I could only dream about how good it must've been when it came across the counter instead of now being a few hours old.

Brandy sat on the navigator's seat next to mine, watching and working on her sandwich as well. Alex and Parker were below at the table, having dinner and discussing family relationship things, I guessed. Glad I was up here, out of earshot.

Sunday night, there wasn't much in the way of traffic, either on our dead-end road or our dead-end creek. Anyone approaching us on either would need to be checked out thoroughly.

Brandy finished her sandwich and came over to stand next to me. "You sure know how to show a girl a good time on her vacation, Reynolds." She squeezed my knee, which she was now also leaning against.

"They don't call me Good Time Danny for nothing!"

"At this rate, I'm going to need some time off to recover from my time off."

"Yeah, sorry about all this. I'd have loved to have turned it over to the cops back in Crozet, but..."

"You couldn't because that might get your card games exposed, and if that happened, your sheriff buddy could get outed, too. I totally get it."

She then checked the breech of the boat's Glock for like the tenth time. I'd swapped it with her for the silenced pistol, and I'd given my Jeep gun to Alex. we'd all agreed that the three of us were going to be the ones to have to do any shooting that might become necessary. Parker was to stay below and out of harm's way.

Like Brandy and me, Alex was very familiar with firearms, but Parker had never been interested in shooting. Hopefully, the Russian wouldn't show up, and if he did, hopefully, we wouldn't need to use our weapons. I'd say that was a fifty-to-one play, at best. Then, I saw headlights pulling into the parking lot. We might be about to test those odds.

Brandy went over to her houseboat while I knocked softly on *Cohiba's* hatch, hearing an answering knock from inside. The hatch slid open slightly, revealing a dark interior. I then joined Brandy, and we silently climbed the stern ladder up to the small flying bridge. Her houseboat was situated bow-in, meaning we had the cover of that fiberglass bridge cowl. Peeking over the edge, we had a perfect view of the dock and *Cohiba's* cockpit. Out of the open back, we could see across the water to the bar and parking lot.

The large SUV stopped several empty spaces away from my Jeep, out of the spill from the lot's sole security light. Apparently, more emphasis was put on securing the boatyard, which had several lights. In this darkness, it was hard to tell exactly what make and color the vehicle was, but I'm willing to bet it was a maroon Caddy. I saw two figures exit the passenger doors, but no interior light came on as they got out. The Russian was here.

Brandy must've come to that same conclusion as she whispered in my ear, "Just in case, I want you to know I love you, Reynolds."

"Ditto."

"Ditto? Really? We've got to work on your communication skills."

"We'll have plenty of time to do that after we take care of things." I paused a minute as we watched those two figures make their way slowly and stealthily past the bar and down the main dock. "Just in case, I love you, too, McDonald."

In the low light coming from the power pedestals placed along every other slip, we could now see that both men had silenced pistols up and at the ready in front of them. The one in the lead held up his free hand when he was close enough to read the name on my boat's stern. Cautiously, they crept closer. One stepped over onto the covering board and began making his way forward, probably going to check to see if the front hatch was unlatched. The other one stepped into the cockpit, facing forward, obviously heading for the hatch.

I yelled, "Drop your weapons!"

The answer I got from the guy on the covering board was a bullet that whizzed past my ear. Brandy and I both opened up on him, and he fell backward into one of those steel support columns, his head making a familiar sound. Alex then began shooting at the second intruder, who had also failed to drop his pistol. That guy managed to get off one shot before crumpling into a heap in the cockpit.

As I stood up and peered across the water at the parking lot, I heard an anguished wail coming from *Cohiba*'s cabin. "Daddy, noooooo!"

I turned toward my boat just as someone hit me in the chest with what felt like a baseball bat. But as I fell toward the deck, I heard the crack of a rifle shot coming from across the water. Just before everything went black, my last thought was: *I'm glad I didn't just leave it at ditto.*

~

FROM THEIR POSITIONS backed into the two overgrown lots across from each other, Tiny and his chief deputy watched as the dark SUV slowly turned right and entered the marina parking lot. Instead of parking under the light at the base of dock, it parked in darkness several spaces over. Tiny's phone vibrated.

"I can't see 'em from here, Sheriff."

"I got 'em, an' they're actin' suspicious, but I don't know if they're the Russkies."

"Shouldn't we go over there?"

Now, the sheriff saw the two guys exit the far side of the vehicle. Both appeared to have long-barreled pistols in their hands. For a brief second, he thought about going over and arresting them, but for all he knew, they had permits for their weapons. Besides, maybe they would shoot Reynolds; then he'd really have a case against them, as well as be finished with Reynolds.

"Naw, hold your position; I don't think they're the ones we're lookin' for."

Several minutes went by, and then there was the unmistakable sound of gunfire. Before he could redial his deputy, he saw a bright muzzle flash coming from the back driver's side window. The SUV then reversed out of the parking space and raced out of the lot. Now Tiny had his deputy on speakerphone. "It's them! Shots fired! They're gonna get away, stop 'em!"

Tiny put his car in drive, but by then, his deputy was already moving to block the narrow street, with his blue lights flashing. The driver of the SUV hit the patrol car back by the trunk, flattening one tire and spinning the vehicle out of his way. Tiny spun his tires as he took off after the fleeing vehicle. He grabbed his radio mic as his speed was increasing. "This is Sheriff Clifford. I'm in pursuit of a maroon Escalade with DC tags. Suspects are armed and danger-ous..." A spiderwebbed hole appeared in his windshield just to the left of his steering wheel. "Suspects are now shootin' at me! We're on the Mobjack Marina Road, headin' for town. I need some goddamn assistance here!"

Tiny's deputy back at the marina radioed, "I'm unable to assist."

"Well, get down ta th' docks an' see if Reynolds is dead. Unit 5, where the hell are you?"

The deputy who had been running radar earlier answered. "I'm in town, Sheriff, and heading your way."

"Naw, you stay there, an' put out some spike strips. Use ah automatic weapons is authorized. Damn, they just shot my car again!"

The radar deputy pulled over next to Ricky's Cafe on the main road. As usual, late on Sunday night, there was no traffic in sight. He pulled out his fully automatic rifle and spike strips from his trunk. Still no traffic in sight, but now he could hear Tiny's siren way off in the distance.

"You ready Unit 5? Crazy sumbitch is doin' over a hundred!"

"Roger that, Sheriff. Spikes are going out now from behind my car. Make sure to stop short." He threw the strip, covering both lanes of the road, then crouched down behind his car with his rifle. Now Tiny's lights were coming into view from way down the road.

A minute later, Tiny spotted the unit off to the side and slammed on his brakes. The driver of the Escalade kept his speed, then lost control when his own windshield became honeycombed with bullet holes. Instead of heading for the spike strips, he veered to the left, hitting the deputy's unit and barrel-rolling sideways down the street before finally coming to rest on its top. Tiny raced over to his deputy to check on him.

"You all right?"

"Yeah. I got 'em, Sheriff!"

"You shore did, son, good work!"

Shots began ringing out from the rear of what was left of the SUV. Tiny cried out in pain as he fell to the street. His deputy turned and began firing on the vehicle again; the spark from one of the bullets hitting the frame ignited the ruptured gas tank, turning the vehicle into an inferno. Screams were heard coming from inside the wreck. They stopped less than a minute later when Uri finally died.

"This is Unit 5; roll an ambo; the sheriff is down! I repeat, officer down! In front of Ricky's Cafe. Also, need fire trucks."

"Dispatch to 5, Roger that. How bad is the sheriff?"

"Ain't good, dispatch."

"Unit 2, I'm at Mobjack Creek Marina and need paramedics and ambos now! Multiple DOAs, and civilians down. I'm need help over here, now!"

EPILOGUE

Have you ever closed your eyes really tight and seen different colors against a black background? That was my world now, along with voices that seemed just out of reach and comprehension. I didn't know how long this had been going on; maybe it was how forever felt? I was guessing I was dead since I couldn't open my eyes. That is, if I still had eyes.

I heard a whirring and clicking sound as slowly a warm feeling washed over my body. My body. I suddenly realized I still had a body, so I couldn't be dead. But I was oh, so tired. Time to sleep.

"How's he doing, Brandy?"

"About the same, Alex. I thought he might be trying to open his eyes a minute ago, but then the morphine pump gave him another dose. I hear you're about to be released, that's great!"

Alex had been rolled in, sitting in a wheelchair pushed by a nurse, who said she would be back in five minutes. His right arm was in a sling. He'd been shot in that shoulder.

"Yes. But I couldn't go without checking on him first. I owe him so much for saving Parker from Aslanov."

"Saved me, too. How do you go about repaying something like that?"

"Seeing as how you haven't left his side for three days, I'd say that kind of devotion is a damn good start."

Parker walked into the room with a bag that she handed to Brandy. "Your boat was locked, but I found these in the hanging locker on *Cohiba*. I figured you'd want some clean clothes. You've got a nice eye for colors, by the way."

"Thanks." Brandy thought: *Parker is trying to make friends; who would've believed it a week ago?*

"Well, Daddy, are you ready to go?"

Brandy asked, "Before you go, have you heard anything about Sheriff Clifford's condition?"

Alex chuckled. "He was released the next day. His was a through-and-through wound to his thigh. No arteries nor bone hit. But was he ever furious when the Feds told him he couldn't say anything about who Uri was. Then he got told the cover story about what happened at the boat as the result of a burglary gone bad, and that didn't help his temperament either. That guy really hates Danny.

"Thanks to those DVDs Danny grabbed off the train, I was able to convince some of my DC associates to track down the rest of the collection and make sure it didn't fall into the wrong hands. I am keeping those three, though. They will help ensure we won't have anything from this bite us in the butt in the future." He winked.

Parker asked, "Please call us when Danny wakes up."

"Sure. And thanks for picking up my clothes."

"Don't mention it," Parker said, thinking: *Those should have been my clothes hanging in that boat. A bartender—really, Danny? You could've had me instead.*

THE MEDICAL EXAMINER put in a call to Tiny. "Sheriff, you know that body we fished out of the water that was part of the marina shootout?"

"Yeah, what about it?"

"I was able to change your cousin Billy's cause of death because of it. It had the same marks on the back of the head as Billy's. Based on the eyewitness accounts, I went back down there and discovered they were caused by falling against a steel 'H' beam column that supports the roof. Billy was so stoned on meth that he lost his balance and fell against one of those same columns next to his boat. It was an accident." He waited to hear a "thank you" or some form of congratulations from Tiny, but instead, he got a torrent of cursing right before Tiny hung up.

"Damn it! That Reynolds is made of Teflon!" Then he thought about what he'd just said and added, "But he ain't quite bulletproof!" He laughed, having last seen Danny with all kinds of tubes and wires connected to him. Then, Tiny accidentally bumped his bullet wound against his desk and began howling in pain.

$\sim$

THE NEXT DAY...

When I opened my eyes, I saw tubes and wires everywhere. And Brandy, asleep in a chair next to me, one of her hands in mine. I twitched involuntarily, and she sat bolt upright, quickly looking at me, relief showing on her face.

"You're awake!"

"Hurts."

"They've been weaning you off the automatic morphine, but if you're in too much pain, you can press this button." She put a button in the hand that had been holding hers. I pressed it and almost instantly felt that warmth again. Realizing I was about to go back to sleep again, I said, "I'm glad we didn't leave it at ditto." The last thing I saw before I passed out was a tear running down Brandy's cheek.

$\sim$

IT TOOK several more days before I was ready to be released. There was no question about where I would be going to rest and recuperate. If you're thinking Crozet, you'd be wrong. Brandy insisted I was going to stay with her on her houseboat.

I had great people taking care of things back in Crozet, and Hitch, Lana, and Luke had all three driven over together not just once but twice to visit me. Yep, great people.

Cam, of course, had visited every day. And yesterday, he'd shown up with a roll of blueprints. It was an architect's design of our new sunset tower. It was another outside bar set on concrete columns, thirty feet up in the air out over the water, right next to the existing dock bar. It even had its own food dumbwaiter and an elevator in addition to stairs.

I said, "I love it! And it's a nice idea there, Walt Disney, but there's no way we can afford to build it."

"We don't have to; it's already been paid for."

"What? How?"

Brandy smiled. "Alex. He said it was a down payment on what he owes you for saving Parker. He and I talked a lot while you were unconscious, and I mentioned our date at Crozet Terrace and how we'd said how neat it would be to have one similar at the Rivah Grill. We met with Cam, and this is what came out of it. What do you think?"

"I think we have a great future ahead. All three of us, and I can't wait."

Brandy grinned. "Ditto."

A FEW NOTES...

While none of the businesses or people included in this book are real, some are based on real people, events, or businesses.

While the media did "out" the Congressional bomb shelter at the Greenbrier in West Virginia, there is **no Presidential bomb shelter** located near Crozet, Virginia—at least, not that we know about. The Charlottesville Regional Airport extended the runway a few years ago to accept larger aircraft, but it didn't seem to have enough traffic to warrant this at the time. However, it wasn't long before the Air Force Special Air Mission group's 757 aircraft (think—the Vice President's usual Air Force 2) began shooting "touch and go" landings there.

Moonrise Brewery—is based on the Starr Hill Brewery in Crozet and the building is next to the tracks, and was a ConAgra food production plant for decades.

The **Tourist Train** is based on the Virginia Scenic Railway (https://www.virginiascenicrailway.com/), which passes through the Blue Ridge Tunnel (https://en.wikipedia.org/wiki/Blue_Ridge_Tunnel) every Wednesday through Sunday afternoon. It's a great trip, especially in the early spring and all through fall.

Amtrak's Chicago to Washington and Washington to Chicago trains do come through every afternoon, and do sometimes pass each other in or near Crozet.

The young, developmentally challenged African-American man who loves watching the trains is a real person. I love seeing him get so much joy out of this.

Mobjack Creek Marina is loosely based on Hudgins Horn Harbor Marina. There's no restaurant or bar there, but I knew when I first visited that I needed to put it in a book. I didn't know then that it would become the central location in a new series.

Mathews, VA is one of my favorite little towns. I've never met the sheriff there, so "Tiny" Clifford is in no way based on any law enforcement officer I've ever met. My apologies to the real sheriff!

About **Ted Clifford**, well, as a former small-town mayor and councilman, Ted is a compilation of many politicians that I met during that period of my life. I'm glad that part of my life is firmly in the rearview mirror.

ABOUT THE AUTHOR

Don Rich is the author of the bestselling Coastal Adventure, Coastal Beginnings, and Mobjack Mystery & Adventure series. Don's books are set mainly in the mid-Atlantic because of his love for this stretch of coastline.

As a fifth-generation Florida native who grew up on the water, he has spent much of his life on, in, under, or beside it. He now makes his home in central Virginia. When he's not writing or watching another fantastic mid-Atlantic sunset, he can often be found in a marina or boatyard somewhere around the Chesapeake Bay or the Atlantic, finding inspiration for his next book.

Don loves to hear from readers, and you can reach him via email at contact@donrichbooks.com

f X ⓞ

ALSO BY DON RICH

As I'm constantly adding new books and series, the best way to keep current with my list is to visit my "Books" page on my website and click on any of the covers for detailed information about that book. https://donrichbooks.com/books/

Made in United States
Orlando, FL
08 May 2025

61127079R00108